You and I Collide

E. A. M. Trofimenkoff

For Coleen & Scott,

You and I Collide

find Joy

EM

First Edition September 2024
Interior Design by Cathrine Swift
Cover Design by E. A. M. Trofimenkoff
Proofread by Rebecca Scharpf

Paperback ISBN: 9781738059768
eBook ISBN: 9781738059775

Also by E. A. M. Trofimenkoff

A Kiss of the Siren's Song (2023)

Cerebral Supernova (Sweet Bitter Love Anthology)

Official Playlist

Somewhere Only We Know — Keane
I Will Follow You into the Dark — Death Cab for Cutie
Collide — Howie Day
You Found Me — The Fray
Carry On — fun.
Count on Me — Bruno Mars
You're My Best Friend — Queen
Cowboy Take Me Away — The Chicks
Don't Go Breaking My Heart — Elton John, Kiki Dee
Here Comes The Sun — The Beatles
Never Say Never — The Fray
I Can See Clearly Now — Jimmy Cliff
Two — Sleeping At Last
dwell on the guilt of saving myself — Super Whatevr
All Through The Night — Sleeping At Last
Only You —Yazoo
I See The Light — Mandy Moore, Zachary Levi
From This Moment On — Shania Twain, Bryan White
Lovebug — Jonas Brothers
After All — Elton John, Charlie Puth
The Last Goodbye — Billy Boyd
Flashlight — Jessie J
Sunday Crossword — J. Maya
Heroe — Il Divo

This playlist is available on Spotify.

DEDICATION

To every broken-hearted dreamer wishing on the stars.

NOTE

There is a crossword puzzle throughout this book. For a
downloadable / printable PDF please visit
www.eamtrofimenkoff.com

Enjoy!

CONTENT WARNING

Some of the content in this book may be distressing to folks who are sensitive to topics regarding the deteriorating health of a loved one. Please take care of yourself, and reach out to a professional should you need it.

This book also contains explicit sexual content and is not recommended for readers under the age of 18.

1 | A | C | R | O | S | S

1

Oh, Chemistry, you are
always on my _ _ _ _ _.

September 20, 2024

My teaching methods may be unorthodox, but there is no
denying that they are effective, especially when I'm standing
on a table with a bucket on top of my head in front of a class
of thirty teenagers who are probably placing bets on whether
or not I make it off of here in one piece.

I reach up and attach the makeshift water stream to the
rod on the roof, and let the roll of paper fall into the metal
bucket. I wince at the clang which now strongly reverberates
in my ears. The students laugh. Good, at least they're paying
attention.

"So, on top of my head is a stream. Think of this as a curtain or waterfall of air that is on top of me at any given time.
Up here, it's not too bad. There's only a small amount on top
of my head." I gesture at the small part of the stream sticking
out on top of the bucket. "But"—I jump down, the bright pink

tips of my long blonde braids flying up with the fall, and say a small thanks to the universe for not rolling my ankle or toppling me over from the action—"down here, there is a much larger stream above my head. That means there is more pressure on the floor than there was on the table. Does that make sense?"

I see a few students appear a bit disappointed, while others look positively triumphant. There are no monetary exchanges under the desks, but I know that will be remedied during class break.

Some of the other students nod, and one overly enthusiastic girl with tight brown curls and big round eyes in the front beams at me. Thank goodness for students that enjoy participating. My job would be so awkward without them. Or maybe it's just me? Maybe I'm awkward. Oh well, it doesn't matter, because if Maggie is the only student to get something out of this lesson, then it was worth it. Having one student understand is always better than zero.

I turn and put the bucket back on the table behind me so I don't have to carry it around on my head anymore.

"Good, so here in Claresholm, we are just over one kilometer above sea level. Would you then expect the atmospheric pressure to be higher or lower here than, say, on the coast of Prince Edward Island?"

Maggie's hand shoots up excitedly. The glow of the early afternoon sun through the window plays across her dark skin. I nod at her to answer the question.

"Lower, because a higher altitude means a lower atmospheric pressure."

I give her a wide smile. "Yes, exactly! And what about say, at the top of Turtle Mountain?"

I look around the room to see if anyone else is brave enough to answer. At the back, Tobe slowly puts up his hand.

He's a shy boy, but he never scored under an A on any of his exams last year, according to his transcript.

Again, I nod, giving him permission to answer.

He swallows and lowers his arm. His classmates turn around, awaiting his answer. His face flushes and he bites at the inside of his cheek. Tobe's eyes dart around from person to person as his hands slowly clench into fists. It's only been a few weeks, but I know his signs. He's uncomfortable. It probably took all of his courage to raise his hand. So, instead of prolonging the silence and forcing him to answer, I give him another option.

"If it's easier, you can point up for a higher atmospheric pressure, or down for a lower atmospheric pressure."

I move my hands up and down to demonstrate what I mean.

Tobe swallows again and then slowly raises his arm to point down with his index finger.

"Wonderful! Thank you, Tobe. You are absolutely correct."

The bell rings, signaling the end of class.

"Don't forget! Your unit exam is next Monday. Happy studying! Remember to drink water and take care of yourselves!" I call after them. Papers shuffle and shoes scuff on the hard linoleum as the class slowly makes their way out the door. Tobe stays behind, still looking down at his desk, tracing the dark lines of the polished wood knots staring back at him.

I can tell from the crease between his brows that he's stuck in some kind of mental loop.

"You did great today, Tobe," I say, trying to reassure him.

He looks up at me, his face an unreadable mask. There's something behind his eyes that I can't quite place. Then he mumbles something under his breath and returns to his desk.

3

I pull up a chair beside him and sit. When I was in high school, I had a friend just like Tobe. She was soft and quiet. She never caused a fuss. One day, the teacher called on her to answer a question even though she hadn't raised her hand to volunteer. It upset Kayla so much that she vomited into her hands. It took her over a week to come back to class, and even then, she sat in the desk closest to the door so she could leave if she had to. I promised myself that day that if I ever became a teacher, I would never subject my students to something like that. After all, why would they trust me to teach them if they couldn't trust me to treat them like a human being?

I adjust my cat-eye glasses and push a stray hair behind my ear. "Do you want to talk about it?" I ask Tobe gently.

He shakes his head from side to side. His soft black locks sway with the motion. His thin frame seems to shrink into his desk even more.

"Okay." Then, because his well-being is much more important than any kind of lecture or information retention, I ask, "Are things okay with your classmates?"

After Kayla had her episode in biology, some of our peers took to calling her names and making faces at her as they passed us in the hallway. In my classroom, my students don't seem to have similar tendencies, but you never know what happens in the halls or after the school day has ended.

Tobe shrugs.

He's as quiet as ever, and I don't want to push him. So instead of pressing any further, I just tell him, "I admit I don't completely understand what it's like to be in your shoes, Tobe. But, for what it's worth, I am willing to try. And, I have known a few people who get nervous when answering questions as well. There are a few strategies I can teach you if you want, or I know some others in the school who have plenty of experience with these things as well."

He looks up at me, his eyes shining with the beginning of tears.

I lean forward and rest my elbows on my knees so I'm closer to his level. "Is that something you think you would like?"

Tobe blinks and swallows, biting the inside of his cheek again.

"You can nod or shake your head if you like. And if this is too much, I won't ask again. But you should know that you're important, Tobe. Your education is important. But, and I want to emphasize this, your health, in all aspects, is the most important, okay?"

Tobe nods.

I give him a warm smile. "Is that a nod for understanding? Or a nod for wanting to learn some tools to help? One finger for the first, two fingers for the second, closed fist for both."

He nods again and holds up a strong fist with one hand as he brushes a stray tear with his other.

I let out a small sigh of relief as feelings of pride and joy swirl around my chest. "Fist bump?" I ask him.

Tobe gives me a small smile and holds out his hand to me. I meet it with my own fist before standing up again.

"Thanks for trusting me, Tobe. And I really hope this helps. I'll call your mom and let her know that you'll be a few minutes late. Can you meet me back here after school?"

"Okay," he says quietly. Then he gathers up his books and makes his way out the door, giving me a shy, yet appreciative smile as he steps out.

A few hours later, we make our way down the hall to the school counselor's office. I knock on Silva's door three times, and she cheerily calls us in. Tobe walks through first after taking a few hesitant steps.

"Come on in, dear!" She turns around in her chair to see me holding the door. "Oh, nice to see you, L!"

I nod my head toward her. "Silva, this is Tobe. Tobe, this is Silva, our school counselor."

She beams at him with a smile fit to light the universe. She was born for this job, and I can't imagine anyone else replacing her.

But she won't be here forever, my mind reminds me, in its typical fashion.

Tobe looks back and forth between me and the petite silver-haired woman apprehensively.

I know that feeling all too well. The first time in an office like this is always daunting. It's terrifying, finding yourself in front of a stranger—trusting them to guide you. It took me nearly a year before I found a therapist that I felt comfortable with. I just hope that Silva is a good fit for Tobe so he doesn't have to go through the same things I did.

"It's lovely to meet you, Tobe. Would you like to sit?" She gestures at an array of chairs in the room. There's a plush yellow loveseat under the window beside the desk, a blue exercise ball, a black leather office chair with a high back similar to the one Silva is sitting in, and a recliner in the corner. If anyone walked in here without checking the name on the door or noticing the posters decorating the walls, they might think that this was some kind of spare chair storage room. But no, this is just how Silva is: accommodating to the very end.

Tobe takes his time looking around, as if choosing the chair will decide his fate. And in a way, it might. Who am I to say it won't?

Eventually he decides on the exercise ball, which is, if I'm being perfectly honest, a bit of a surprise. But the effect is immediate. His shoulders relax, and the crease between his eyebrows smooths.

I take a deep breath and run my hands down my jeans before bringing them back up and lacing my fingers together.

E. A. M. Trofimenkoff

"How are you feeling, Tobe?" I ask him.

He bounces up and down a few times before giving me a thumbs-up.

"Great. Okay. I guess my job here is done then." I turn around and Silva follows me to the door.

Before I leave, I make sure to give him a thumbs-up in return.

"Good luck, Tobe. I'll see you on Monday."

The last thing I hear before Silva shuts the door behind me is "So, Tobe. L tells me you're in their chemistry class, is that right?"

The hallways are empty, and only the sound of my echoing footsteps on the hard white floor accompanies me. During the day I almost forget how empty it can feel roaming around the school by myself. I'm almost back to my classroom when my phone beeps in my pocket. The screen lights up with a call from Mom.

"Hello?" I answer.

"L?" Mom's voice cracks on the other side of the line.

"Mom? Is everything okay?"

There's a long silence before she replies, and my stomach tightens into a knot.

"You need to come home."

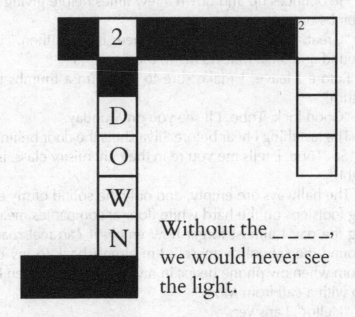

2

2

D
O
W
N

Without the _ _ _ _,
we would never see
the light.

September 20, 2024

I told you something bad was going to happen, my brain
gremlins tell me.

*Yes, well, you always think something bad is going to hap-
pen, so you're eventually going to be right. A broken clock
tells the right time twice a day, remember?* I retort back, although it sounds suspiciously more like Iris, my therapist, in
my head than my own voice.

He's probably already dead.

You've missed saying goodbye to him. Just like last time.

Too bad you're selfish and work all the time.

"Shut up!" I yell.

I throw my keys in my purse and leave my desk in the disaster state it's in as I rush out, pushing the door straight into someone.

I don't know if I blacked out for a second, but all of a sudden, I'm on my hands and knees, which are screaming at me in pain.

"Fuck," a low voice grunts from behind me.

I turn around to see a man holding a hand to the side of his head. His dark hair is pulled back into a bun, but a stray strand hangs down over his fingers. "Are you okay?"

It takes me a second to register that he's asking me if I'm okay, despite the fact that I just ran him over with a door.

My phone pings again.

Shit.

"I-I'm sorry," I stammer. "I have to go."

I grab my purse from the ground, and without a second glance back, proceed to race out the door and into the parking lot.

As I scramble to find my keys in the now completely disorganized pack I call a purse, my mind races. Was that a literal hit-and-run? Can I be sued for that? No one would really sue someone for accidentally hitting them with a door, right?

I take a deep breath and focus on the rough asphalt under my shoes. I grind one foot in, taking care to listen to the sound of it before stepping behind the wheel. Despite my efforts to ground myself, I can't shake the hurricane of worst-case scenarios playing through my head.

The short five-minute drive back to my house feels like a lifetime. As if the street in front of me is stretching out faster than I'm moving down it. But the clock never lies. And okay, so maybe I sped a little and made it in four minutes instead of five, but the point is I got here. And I barely remember anything after fastening my seatbelt and driving down the eternally stretching fourth street. So, in a way, it's a bit of a miracle I made it here in the first place.

My parents' silver car is parked in the driveway. All of the lights are on in the house. I see a few shadows moving behind the curtains in the window as I climb the stairs up to the door. I barely have my fingers wrapped around the handle before it's pulled open by my dad.

"Hey, bud."

I wrap my arms around him and bury my face in his chest as if I'm a child again. He gently closes the door behind me because he knows that Nox, one of my beautiful black cats, likes to test her luck at being an escape artist. And, perhaps more importantly, he knows that I can be a bit over-the-top when it comes to open doors and windows.

"Was it Pops?" I ask, scared to know the answer. My voice is muffled by his shirt.

"He's stable for now."

Dad holds me tight. He used to be hesitant about these kinds of embraces, but after thirty years, he's had no choice but to warm up to them.

"They shipped him up to the Rockyview. The ambulance picked him up about ten minutes ago. Your mom went by to drop off some biscuits and found him on the ground. It couldn't have been very long—the coffee that spilled from his mug was still hot. Although"—he pauses—"you might need to get him a new rug."

I don't know when I started crying, but there's a damp spot on Dad's shirt that soaks into my cheek as I let out a soft laugh.

"I don't care about the rug, Dad."

"I know," he says before letting me go.

I wipe my face with the back of my hands and suck in a shaky breath.

"I ?" Mom calls from the kitchen.

10

Dad steps to the side, letting me through. I let my purse fall to the ground. It's chaos in there anyway. I'll deal with it later.

Mom stands by the island, her salt-and-pepper hair pulled back into a braid. Her apron is sideways, making her look like she has her weight perched on one hip while still managing to stand up straight. I wrap my arms around her too, taking in her warm scent of cinnamon and chocolate.

"You okay?" I ask her.

She nods her head into my shoulder. "I will be. You?"

"I will be," I echo. "What do we do now?"

Mom is the first to pull away from our hug, and I already feel an emptiness settling in my body.

"Your uncle offered to meet them at the hospital and let us know when your grandfather is settled into a room or if they run any tests right away. There's not a lot we can do for now though. Unless you want to go up instead?"

I look over to Dad, who's holding a set of keys in his hand. I know that if I asked him, he would drive us all up to Calgary in a heartbeat. And I'd be lying if I said it wasn't a tempting offer.

I find myself nodding. "I think I'd like to go."

"I'll start the car."

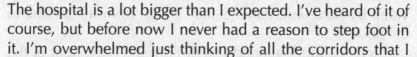

The hospital is a lot bigger than I expected. I've heard of it of course, but before now I never had a reason to step foot in it. I'm overwhelmed just thinking of all the corridors that I could accidentally get lost in.

"Harry Tenduil," Mom says to the woman behind the information desk, and then she spells out Pops' last name.

After a few clicks, the woman's short brown curls bounce as she nods.

"He's been admitted, but is still in the emergency room. If you follow the signs to your left, you should find your way there easily." Her voice is high and chipper, like she's giving us directions to the nearest gas station, not the emergency wing of a hospital.

"Thank you."

We follow the signs and find ourselves in a large white room filled with occupied chairs. There are at least a dozen people with round containers in front of them that I can only assume are meant for vomit. Several others have crying children, and one gentleman in the corner is pale and slouched over. Just when I'm about to suggest that someone take a look at him, he jolts back awake and glances nervously around the room.

His sudden movement is enough for me to nearly jump out of my shoes. I guess I'm more on edge than I thought.

A nurse leads us past the admittance doors to a long hallway lined with the same wooden doors adorned with medical charts. The smell of cleaning products makes my stomach turn, and I force myself to breathe through my mouth to stop my nose from burning.

"Here we are," the petite dark-skinned woman says before turning around again, responding to some kind of alarm that just began to ring. The knot of hair on top of her head bounces as she makes her way back to the nurse's station.

Mom takes my hand and guides me into the room. It's divided by pale blue curtains that stretch from the ceiling to the floor.

There's a loud, gurgled cough from the back right of the room that I would recognize anywhere. My feet suddenly feel much more planted on the ground, as if before I was just coasting, floating along, going through the motions, but now I'm solid. Tangible. Real. I'm here. And so is he.

"Pops?"

My feet move before I give a conscious demand for them to do so.

"L?"

I peer behind the curtain to find him lounging on his bed with his arms behind his head and that familiar quirky smile plastered across his face.

"Good to see ya, kid. What brings ya to my neck of the woods?"

I roll my eyes. "You know, if you wanted an all-inclusive stay somewhere, all you had to do was ask."

He winks at me, and I find peace as we settle into our familiar banter.

"Nah, what fun would that be?"

"Good to see you in high spirits, Dad," Mom says as she leans over to give him a kiss on the head.

The fluffy short white hair around his bald cul-de-sac stands up at awkward angles from his head, making him look surprised and disheveled, which I guess he probably is. Mom tries to push it down, but her efforts are futile.

"Your hair—"

"Has a mind of its own," Pops interrupts, which earns him a stern glance from Mom. "I am Harry, after all."

"Ha-ha," Mom replies, sarcastically. "Tell that to your vacant island."

"Hey, you leave my island out of this." He wags a finger at her, and I notice that his skin looks a bit paler than usual. "Like I said, mind of its own. I don't make the rules."

The blood pressure machine beside him beeps as it starts to take his next measurement.

"Damn thing won't let me have a minute's peace," Pops grumbles.

"Harold Tenduil?" a low voice says from behind the curtain.

"If he's here, then I really am dead."

13

Mom elbows Pops and he lets out a low, throaty laugh.

"What? Too soon to make jokes like that, Rotha?"

"I see you still have your sense of humor—that's a good thing," the doctor says as he steps inside our little cubicle. He's holding a wooden clipboard in his hands, presumably with Pops' information on it. I can't help the rush of nerves that run through my body as I study the doctor and his reaction to reading whatever it is on those pages. Even more frustrating, he doesn't let a hint of anything show through his professional mask.

His dark hair is pulled back into a tight bun at the top of his head, giving an angular shape to his deep brown eyes. There's a fine line that is permanently creased on his forehead. For a moment, I wonder how many patients live in that small crevice on his brown skin. How many of them were lost? And would my Pops one day contribute to that as well?

"I'm Doctor Kawatha, and I'll be taking care of you during your stay here. So, Harold—"

"Please, doc, call me Harry," Pops interrupts.

"Harry," the doctor affirms, "how are you feeling right now? Any pain, numbness, or dizziness?"

Pops shakes his head. "I feel fine."

"Hmm . . . " Doctor Kawatha murmurs. "It says here that you had a fall and were found unconscious in your room, is that correct?"

Pops swallows nervously and finally nods.

"Okay, well, that is concerning," the doctor admits. "What is the last thing you remember before falling?"

Pops and Mom exchange a glance, leaving me with only my imagination to hear the unsaid words between them.

"I was on the phone with my daughter, Rotha," he says, pointing at Mom.

"And did you feel anything unusual during this conversation leading up to your fall?" the doctor asks as he scribbles something down on the page.

"Not really. I woke up late and missed breakfast. Rotha said she would bring me over some biscuits and muffins instead. I was on my way to the kitchen to fetch myself a coffee when . . . well, you know the rest I guess."

"Uh-huh."

Doctor Kawatha makes a few more notes before looking back up at the rest of us.

"It is possible that Harry here just had a dizzy spell due to low blood sugar, but just to make sure, we're going to run a few tests to rule out some of the more serious issues. Harry"—the doctor turns toward Pops—"we're going to have to keep you here for a few days until we're certain this was just a one-time thing. Especially since you lost consciousness. We want to make sure you don't have anything else happening in that clever brain of yours."

Pops gives him one of his charming, crooked smiles. "As long as there's Jello on demand, I guess I can make that work."

I roll my eyes.

It's the one good thing about hospitals: Jello without any of the work or waiting.

I hear the words in my mind just as clearly as if he were to say them to me right here.

"Thank you, doctor," Mom says.

"It's my honor," Doctor Kawatha says before turning around and leaving us.

A nurse follows quickly behind with a fresh IV bag. "Hi everyone!" he says, full of energy despite the time. He nudges between us to fiddle with the standing bar beside Pops. "This should help you feel better, Harry."

"Five-star service!" Pops teases and we all let out a shut-tered laugh. "Y'all should go," he says. "You look tired, and I'm fine. I promise I'm not going anywhere."

Although I'm relieved from seeing him and the doctor, there's a pit in my stomach that won't quite dissolve.

"I'm glad you're in good hands," I tell him as I lean over and give him a hug.

"You know me," he says, a hint of mischief in his voice. "As long as they're warm, who am I to complain?"

"You're hopeless."

Mom rolls her eyes as she too gives him a hug good-night.

"Take care, Harry," Dad says from the corner.

"I love you all very much," Pops replies, but his eyes stay fixed on mine. There's a familiar tenderness carried through his words.

"Now, time to go!" he says, waving his hands toward the end of his bed. "Seriously, what does a man have to do to get some beauty sleep around here?"

He gives us a playful smirk.

Mom takes my hand, and just with that one simple ges-ture, I feel grounded. The floor is under my feet again, and the buzzing in my ears lessens.

He's in good hands, I remind myself. *He's still here. And if nothing else, at least you got to say goodbye.*

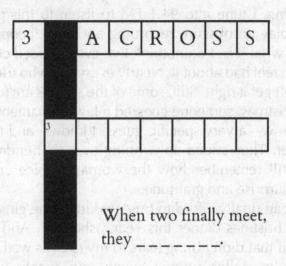

3 | A | C | R | O | S | S

When two finally meet,
they _ _ _ _ _ _ _ .

September 23, 2024

One of the nurses called to let us know they would be keeping Pops through the week since they needed to run some more tests, and the technicians weren't available until the middle of the week. Something about mitigating risks . . . Mom and Dad went up to visit him again, but I had to stay behind to prepare for the next week's worth of lectures and my students' unit exam. We FaceTimed while they were there, which I was thankful for, but there isn't anything that can truly substitute a face-to-face visit and a warm hug from your favorite person on the planet.

I turn the radio on as I wait for Charlie, my Nissan Rogue, to warm up. It's surprisingly cold for the end of September, and I can't help but be nervous for what that means the winter will be like once it eventually arrives.

"The Elusive Echo . . ." an ominous voice says. Every morning, I tune into 94.1 FM to listen to this game where they play an obscure recording and have people call in to guess what it is. I don't think I've ever guessed correctly, but I don't feel bad about it. Nearly everyone who tries to answer doesn't get it right. Still, some of the sounds are fun. Last year at Christmas, someone guessed a lawn ornament falling into the snow—a very specific guess, I know—and that was the answer. They ended up winning over six hundred dollars. I can still remember how the woman's voice cracked from pure surprise and gratitude.

"I can finally afford to buy my kids some gifts and have a real Christmas dinner this year," she said. And I would be lying if that didn't bring tears to my eyes as well.

"Hello, caller number twenty-one, what's your name?" Sully, the radio host, asks.

There's some static on the other end before a soft voice with a southern twang answers.

"You can call me anything you like, hun, as long as you don't call me late for dinner."

An echo of laughs fills the car. And it's almost like I'm not alone.

"The name's Georgia, if you must know. Now, are we ready to play this thing or what?"

Sully lets out a low chuckle into his microphone.

"You know, I like you, Georgia. Good luck."

I rub my hands together trying to warm them up as I listen. If I'm being perfectly honest, it sounds just like all of the other ones. Like a drawer closing or something solid falling. It's almost impossible to decipher the sounds, which makes for a good game, I suppose.

"Hmmm . . ." Georgia says, "I think it's the lid of a coffee maker closing. You know, like where you put the grounds?"

A seconds passes before the classic defeat motif plays, signaling that this is the incorrect answer.

"Sorry, Georgia, that was a great guess, but unfortunately not the right one. Stay tuned for another opportunity to guess the Elusive Echo tomorrow morning with Sully. Have a bright sunshining day!"

The program switches back to the classic rock music that typically plays on the station throughout the day. The song this time? "Sultans of Swing" by Dire Straits. I turn up the volume as I pull out of the driveway and make my way to the school.

There are a few cars in the parking lot by the time I arrive, but it's still empty for the most part. I do notice however, that someone has parked in the spot that I usually use. We don't have designated parking places, but after five years of consistently parking in the same stall, I figured it had my invisible name on it.

"Ugh," I groan, rolling my eyes for good measure. Maybe the universe really does have it out for me. And then again, maybe this is just a stupid parking space and I should get over it. I choose pettiness. Something other than caffeine needs to fuel me through this day anyway. I pull in beside the Silverado, parking on its passenger side. It's closer to the school entrance, but it still feels wrong. I sincerely hope this isn't going to be a sign for how my day is going to go.

Once again, the school is quiet without the hustle of students in the halls. It can sometimes feel spooky, especially when I arrive in the dark during the winter months, but now while the sun is up bright and early still, it's more peaceful than anything else. I'm almost at my classroom when I realize I forgot the exams in Charlie.

I let out a long sigh, drop off my bags outside my class-room door and make my way back to my car. The back door on the drivers side always needs a little extra jiggle before opening, and this time is no exception. Unfortunately, as I grab the exams from the back seat, one of them topples to the floor, and I'm forced to awkwardly lean over to reach it. My keys fall from my coat pocket onto the ground outside Charlie, and once again I let out a groan of frustration. I try to remind myself that things happen in threes, so hopefully we have taken all of them into account by now, and that means the rest of the day will be smooth sailing.

"Hey, I think you dropped—"

I jolt in surprise from the voice behind me and end up hitting the car door with my ass in the process. Now, this wouldn't usually be a problem. A hazard of having an above average size backside is that you tend to hit it on things every now and again. This is, as I probably should have known, not a usual day, nor are these usual circumstances. So rather than the car door just bumping out a little further, I turn around just in time to watch it collide with the same man I hit-and-ran only three days ago right between the eyes.

"Fuck," he groans.

Is this déjà vu? Or Groundhog Day? Am I cursed? Is he cursed? Oh god, is my ass cursed?

Mortified, I turn around the rest of the way and get out of the car.

This is hugely embarrassing. Not only have I physically injured this man twice, but this time it was a by-product of having hips that don't lie.

"Oh shit," I finally say as I close the door. "Are you okay?"

He holds up his hand to his forehead. There's already a thin red line beginning to form, made worse from the cold air around us.

"Is this a habit of yours?"

I pinch my brows together as I readjust my hold on the exams in my arms.

"Is what a habit?"

"Hitting people with doors?"

The constant whirring in my head stops for a second. A playful smirk tugs at the corners of his lips. The ball of his lip ring shifts out slightly as he runs his tongue along his lower teeth, presumably inspecting for any further damage.

"Do I at least get to know the name of the cause of my concussion?"

That takes me aback.

"Uh . . ."

"Your name is Uh?" he teases.

I roll my eyes at him. "No."

I have no idea what's happening here. Am I the one with the concussion? Oh no, is this a real hit-and-run? No. Not this time. I'm not running. Quite the opposite. I seem to be completely frozen in place. Emphasis on the frozen. Seriously, did Mother Nature turn down the thermostat or what?

The man looks at me expectantly, one eyebrow slightly raised. Finally, I find my voice.

"My name is L with no E's, like the letter. And I use they/them pronouns."

He seems satisfied with that.

"Well, L with no E's, I'm Ashe, with an E. He/him."

I blink a few times, trying to put the letters together. Ash with an E?

"Eash . . ." I mumble trying to sound it out.

"What?" he asks.

I look up at him, confused.

There's a long moment of silence before something clicks behind his eyes and he starts laughing.

"Oh, no, it really is pronounced like ash, like the snow-flakes of fire. The E is at the end."

Like the snowflakes of fire. What a beautiful sentiment. I might have to use that some time.

"Ashe, well, it's nice to meet you, and, uh, sorry about the whole hitting you with doors thing."

He shrugs. "I've got a hard head. I'll be fine."

A nervous laugh escapes my chest, which comes out as more of a croak than anything else.

Doubly embarrassed, I turn to make my way back to the school.

"Forgetting something?" Ashe asks.

I pause to take a quick inventory of everything I have in my arms. Purse? Check. Exams? Check. Phone? In my pocket. So what is it?

I turn around to find Ashe with the key to Charlie hanging off his index finger.

"Oh, thanks," I say nervously as I reach out my pinky for him to place the keyring around. His pinky just brushes past mine as he hands them over, sending fire coursing through my veins. Suddenly it's not so cold outside anymore.

"No problem," he says. "Thanks for the headache."

"Everyone says I'm good for that," I blurt out, and if I wasn't before, now I am definitely planning on burrowing myself in a hole and hibernating until I become a fossil because I'm not quite sure how I have been allowed to function in society, let alone participate and engage in it.

"I doubt that," he replies, leaning his head to the side slightly.

"Are you sure that's not your concussion talking?"

He thinks about that for a second.

When did we start walking back to the school? We're almost at the door when he quickly steps in front of me to grab the handle.

"Don't want to risk it again." He gives me a sideways grin as he opens the door and gestures for me to go through first.

The movement seems vaguely familiar.

"Oh, I think we've met before."

A flash of concern crosses his face.

"Are you sure you're not the one who's concussed?" he asks.

I shake my head. "No, on the first day of school, you held the door for a bunch of us as we were bringing things in to set up."

I have no idea why that image is permanently ingrained in this silly brain of mine, but I see it clear as day in my mind's eye. Ashe, holding the door in his Orbit Culture band T-shirt, one hand fiddling with the bottom hem, with his black skinny jeans and Vans, his hair tied up in a bun on top of his head, the black metal of his nose and lip piercings reflecting the early morning sun. Something stirs in me at the memory. I don't usually recall those kinds of interactions—if you can even call it that. But this was like a perfect moment frozen in time that is immortalized in my mind. Then again, maybe it's nothing. I'm probably overthinking it like I do everything in my life. Especially considering everything going on.

"Well?" Ashe asks.

"What?"

We're somehow at the door of my classroom, Ashe looking down at me with his hand outstretched.

"Do you have your classroom key? I'll open it for you since your hands are full."

I brush off the mental cobwebs that had started to accumulate in my mind and tell myself to take a freaking breath. It's barely eight o'clock and I'm wound up tighter than a jack-in-a-box. Do they still make those?

Focus, I tell myself.

I take a breath and twist to my right.

"Lanyard on my purse zipper. Bronze key that looks like it has a lightning bolt engraved on it."

Ashe removes the lanyard, finds the key, and opens the door to my home away from home.

"Well, this is me," I say as if he's walking me home from a night out.

Yeah, that's pretty fucking obvious, the gremlins reply.

I immediately scold myself. Seriously, who let me graduate to the rank of adult again?

Ashe gives me a playful smile and puts my keys on top of the exams in my arms.

"Have a good day, L."

"You too, uh, you do good at . . . you know." I realize I have no idea why this man is at the school in the first place? Is he a teacher? No. I've never seen him in the lunchroom. But he clearly knows his way around.

Embarrassed and unsure of how to get out of the situation, I say the one thing that comes to my mind that everyone does all day every day. "Have fun metabolizing oxygen and exhaling carbon dioxide!"

Yeah, I'll take that hibernation hole right about now.

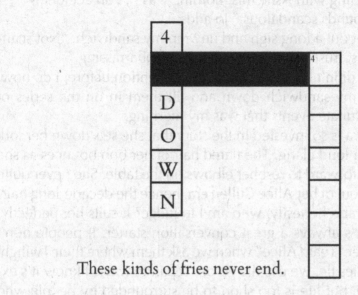

These kinds of fries never end.

September 23, 2024

"Did my eyes betray me, or did I see you walk in with a certain handsome lad this morning?" Jo raises a blonde eyebrow at me. The corner of their lips turn up slightly into a smirk.

"I didn't know you were seeing anyone, L!" Mira says as she looks up from her mason jar salad. "When did that start? And who? And more importantly, *a man*?"

I shake my head and wave my hand in front of me, dismissing their comments as I take my seat at our personal staff room lunch table. "No, I'm not seeing anyone. You three would be the first to know."

I scan my eyes over my friends, Jo, Mira, and Vic, who is silently sipping their tea at the end of the table, watching everything unfold. Their short dark curls fall into their eyes slightly as they study me over their glasses. "And," I continue, "the thing with Ashe this morning was . . . an accident?"

"Sounds scandalous," Jo adds.

I let out a long sigh and unwrap my sandwich. "Not scandalous, trust me. But it was plenty embarrassing."

If I didn't have their undivided attention before, I do now. I put my sandwich down and fill them in on the series of unfortunate events that was my morning.

Mira is so invested in the story that she sets down her fork with a loud clang. The flared hair of her bob bounces as she leans forward to rest her elbows on the table. She never quite grew out of her Alice Cullen era, hence the decade-long hairstyle, and honestly, who am I to judge? It suits her perfectly, and it's always a great conversation starter. If people don't answer "Team Alice" when we ask them where their Twilight loyalties lie, we usually go our separate ways. I know it's extreme, but life is too short to be surrounded by people who are . . . well . . . wrong. The only better test of compatibility is what people choose as their favorite Gandalf quote.

"Did you kiss? They always kiss in the movies." Mira basically swoons off her chair, hands tucked daintily under her chin, eyes looking up as if daydreaming.

"You are a hopeless romantic," Vic says after taking a long sip of their tea.

"There's always hope when it comes to love." Jo leans over and places a gentle kiss on Vic's cheek. Despite their obvious efforts to conceal it, a pink blush covers their face.

Not for the first time, I find myself overwhelmed with a warm feeling of happiness for the two of them. They met at a midnight showing of *Shakespeare in Love* a few years ago and never looked back. I don't think they've ever exchanged a gift that wasn't related to the film in some kind of way. Puns, quotes, merchandise, you name it. One day, there will be a museum devoted to their love for each other and the 1998 movie. It will be one for the history books.

"You were saying about the kissing?" Vic says, trying to move the attention from them.

I shake my head. "No kissing."

I bite into my sandwich and cover my mouth while I continue. I know it's rude to chew with your mouth full, but we only get a thirty-five minute lunch, so we need to make the most of every second. "I don't need any distractions right now anyway."

The three of them nod, but none of them seem completely convinced.

"Any news?" Vic asks.

I drop my gaze as I chew. I know I don't have to keep up a strong façade with my friends, but I don't want to burden them. They have enough going on in their own lives. Plus, it's not like any of us can do anything at this point.

"Just waiting on some tests. Should hopefully have some answers by the end of the week."

Jo eyes me curiously. "You sure you're doing okay, L?"

I straighten my shoulders and raise my chin. "Yeah, just tired, you know? Spent all weekend preparing for lectures this week and printing exams for today."

"L . . ."

I wrap up the empty Ziploc bag and put it back in my lunch kit. "I promise I'm okay." I open my eyes wide and put a smile on my face. For extra emphasis, I lean forward and tilt my head slightly to the side. This seems to pacify them for now. Good. I hate it when people worry about me. That energy could be spent in much better ways, directed toward people who need it a lot more than I do.

"Hey, did you hear about—"

Mira is abruptly cut off as the door to the lunch room opens, revealing a completely lost-in-his-own-world Ashe holding some kind of spray bottle in one hand, and a cloth in the other. My mouth goes dry when our eyes meet, and my face begins to heat. Am I coming down with something? Is it a virus? A fever? Something worse? I can't afford to get sick given everything happening in my life. I make a mental note to pick up some extra Vitamin C and D before going home after work tonight.

"Ashe?" I blurt.

All eyes turn to the man in the doorway.

He blinks a few times, as if struck by something, before his system reboots and he finally acknowledges us.

"Hi, sorry, I hope I'm not interrupting."

Mira and Jo exchange a glance before they turn their attention to me. My face heats even further. I'm starting to think Vitamin C won't be enough. Better pick up some Vicks while I'm at the pharmacy as well.

"No, not interrupting," I say, perhaps a little too quickly. "Uh . . . What's up?"

What's up? my gremlins scold me. They're right, of course. Who am I? One of my fifteen-year-old students?

Ashe holds up his bottle with one hand while the other pulls at the front of his shirt. "Just making my rounds. I can come back though. I didn't realize this was one of the staff lunchrooms."

It's not officially, but we commandeered it when we all needed a place to escape to after they hired Walter to teach social studies. He didn't last long, but we stayed in our cozy nook anyway. It's technically a drama room, but they only ever use it as a changeroom for performances, so it's usually empty.

Mira looks back and forth between Ashe and me with almost an expectant expression on her face.

"Oh! Ashe, these are my friends, Mira, Jo and Vic. Y'all, this is Ashe with an E."

And why the hell did I just introduce him like that? Maybe I *am* sick, because something is clearly not well with me.

"We just met this morning. Well, I guess we met last Friday after I ran him over. Not with my car though. With the door. And not my car door, with the door of my classroom. I ran into him with my car door this morning."

And then I shut my mouth before something else comes out of it like "and we definitely didn't kiss after it happened." Curse you, Mira, for putting those thoughts in my head.

He gives a slight nod to each of them. "Pronouns?" he asks.

"She/her," Mira says.

Jo gestures to both themself and Vic before answering. "We're thembo's just like L here."

Ashe nods again, but doesn't take his eyes off me. I can't help but stare back. In the low amber light of the room, his golden skin seems to glow. His mouth parts slightly as he runs his tongue along the soft skin of his lower lip, catching the black ring on the way by.

A loud buzz breaks me out of my trance. Lunch is over. Class starts again in five minutes.

"Well, I'll let you all get back to it," Ashe says, holding the door for us as we stand to leave.

"Thanks," I say as I walk past him, avoiding his gaze. But all I can think is "saved by the bell."

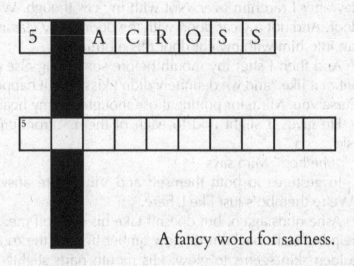

5 ACROSS

A fancy word for sadness.

September 23, 2024

Students are already starting to pour into the classroom and I haven't even put the exams out yet. I basically throw my lunch kit into my bag and grab the stack of papers from the bottom drawer of my desk.

The low, anxious chitter of voices creates a white noise that sets my teeth on edge as I pass out the tests, placing them face down on each student's desk. When I get to the front, I notice Maggie's complexion has turned startlingly pale. She fiddles with a ring around her finger, spinning the inner part over and over and over again. Her eyes are focused on something far away, possibly not even in this dimension.

"Everything okay?" I ask her softly.

Maggie jolts as if waking up from a dream of falling. She nods slightly, and even though her attention is back to the classroom, she still turns the ring with her thumb. "I just get a little nervous about exams," she confesses.

I understand. I used to be like that as well.

"Me too," I tell her. Sometimes all you need is to know you're not alone in your struggles.

I give her a soft smile as I move on to the next desk. Once all of the tests have been given out, I turn around and address the class.

"Okay folks, you have just over an hour to complete this unit exam. Please don't leave any questions blank. I can't mark what I can't see. So even if you're not sure on what to do, here are a few good starting points."

I take out my Expo pen and write a list of three things for the students to consider.

"First, calculate the molar mass and convert your grams to moles," I say as I write. "Next, write a balanced equation. And finally, write down a formula you think applies to this kind of problem. Even if it's a conversion factor."

I turn back around to face them and readjust my glasses. There are a few students itching to start, but most of them look nervous, tired, or worse, uninterested.

I guess we'll see how this goes, I think to myself. The first exam is always the weirdest. I say weirdest because it's not always the worst in the way that people think. It's a learning opportunity for them, the students, but also for me as their teacher. It lets me know where things went well, and perhaps more importantly, where things didn't. It's as much a tool of evaluation for them as it is for me.

"Any last questions before we get started?"

I take a quick look around the class, and when no one raises their hand, I tell them to get started.

When I return to my desk, my phone lights up with a text message from Iris, my therapist.

Hi, L,
This is just a message to remind you about our appointment today at 4:30 p.m. Looking forward to seeing you then.

Honestly, thank the Universe for Iris. At least one of us has our shit together, and it sure as hell isn't me. I send her a short note back confirming my appointment, and bring my attention back to my students before I remember that it's been a whole month since I've journaled anything. I haven't even touched the thing since my last appointment with her.

I grind my teeth together. I used to be so good at this at the beginning, always writing down and documenting everything. Sometimes I would even make little drawings in my notebook if I was inspired to do so. And now look at me. I'm failing at therapy. Can you even fail therapy? Maybe I should just text her back and cancel. What do I even have to talk about anyway?

Turns out the answer to that question is "a lot." As soon as the hypothetical pops into my head, a thousand answers come to mind. Too many to sort through. There always is.

The class is quiet, save for the scratches on the paper. So, just like when I am preparing to go to the dentist by flossing two hours before my appointment, I bring out my journal from my bag and write down a last-minute entry. It's more of a bullet point list, really, but hopefully it will do the job. Maybe I won't completely flunk out. D is still a pass, right? Do therapists grade you? Would that even be ethical? A part of me almost thinks that would be counterproductive, considering the nature of the environment, but you never know. Better to be safe than sorry. And I can't afford to be a disappointment to anyone else.

I look up every few words to make sure my students don't have any questions. No hands are raised throughout the entire exam. The list in front of me turns into a few paragraphs, and before I know it, I have an entire essay on my life of the last thirty days.

There, I think to myself, *that should be good enough*.

The bell rings, signaling the end of class. Chairs scrape against the floor as my students collect their bags and stand up to leave.

"You can leave your tests face down. Enjoy the rest of your day!" I call after them.

When everyone has left, I gather up the papers into a neat stack and place them on top of my desk. I have a prep period now, thankfully, so I decide to use that time to mark the exams. As I press play on my piano concerto marking playlist, I quickly fall into the grounded and peaceful mindset that I always adopt before grading exams.

Roran does well, scoring a solid 84%. It's a great start, and an invisible weight lifts from my shoulders. Just as I accept the feeling of pride into my body, I move on to Maggie's exam. The feeling of pride is completely washed away when I see that it is completely blank. And not just the first page. The entire exam. Not a single answer to be seen. Not even a hint of a word or calculation. Nothing.

Suddenly I can't help but think that maybe I shouldn't have been so worried about failing as a therapist's patient. Maybe I should have been worried about failing as a teacher.

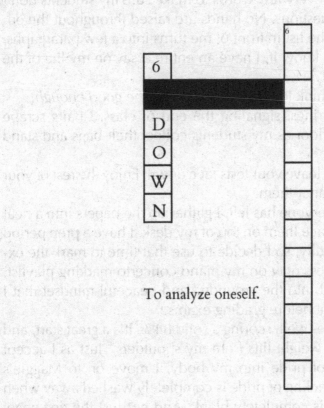

To analyze oneself.

September 23, 2024

Iris' office hasn't changed at all in the last three years I've been seeing her. At first, I wasn't too sure about the pale-yellow walls, but they've grown on me. Now when I walk in, it feels like getting a small dose of evening sky, which was probably the point all along—I just wasn't well enough to understand it at first.

The large painted tree behind her chair will always be my favorite part of the room. It covers the entire wall from floor to ceiling. Its branches stretch out across the width as if ready to embrace anyone and everyone in a warm rainbow hug. The trunk is a matte black, but each of the main six branches stemming from it are their own solid color. Each smaller branch is a muted hue of its parent, making it look almost like a watercolor painting. And at the end of every branch is an emotion. When I first started seeing Iris, I was almost exclusively in the blue sadness section, but as I've learned and grown, I've found myself having moments of green and yellow in my day-to-day life. Learning to accept the brighter colors into what used to be a seemingly endless pool of darkness has been a trial all of its own. I nearly fell out of my chair when she told me that it was possible to feel peaceful and optimistic without also always anticipating the next episode that would inevitably end it. It's a work in progress, but every small step counts. At least that's what she tells me.

Iris walks in and I sit up straighter on the gray couch. She closes the door behind her and slides the label on the door indicating that she is in a session with a patient.

"Hi, L," she says as she takes her seat in front of the tree. "What color are you feeling today?" It's the same question every time, which is honestly a relief. I always know what to expect . . . at the start, anyway.

I pinch my lips to the side as I consider her question. What color am I feeling today? I look back and forth between the branches, trying to find the perfect one that resonates with me. Iris picks up on my efforts almost immediately.

"Description, not perfection. There's always nuance."

I nod. Again, almost a constant reminder she has to give me. There is almost never a perfect answer to any question, much less about things that are extremely difficult to describe for those of us who have forced down our emotions our whole lives.

"Orange, I think," I finally say.

Iris turns around in her chair to inspect the wall. "Any particular branch?"

She trails her fingers along the ends of each one. "Tell me when one feels right," she instructs.

When she lands on "nervous," I stop her.

"It's been a long week," I try to explain, but then immediately feel foolish. It's only Monday.

Iris just nods. "Yes, some days can feel much longer than others," she says understandingly as she turns back and opens her file on me. "What's the first thing that comes to mind when I say 'nervous'?"

An image of my Pops immediately flashes through my mind. He's hooked up on tubes, chest no longer rising and falling. There's a loud, sustained noise in the background as his heartbeat completely stops.

"Pops," I tell her, because there's no use in lying.

"And is it just him as a person? Or something else?"

I take a deep breath and tell her about the vision in my brain that I can't seem to get rid of. Tears sting at the edges of my eyes, and I blink trying to get rid of them before they fall in an uncontrollable flood down my cheeks.

Iris sets down her pen. "Is it the same as before?"

The same as before. The words echo in my head. No? But also yes? It feels like the same melody of a song being played over a new setting. It's haunting and familiar. But not necessarily the same as it was three years ago when I basically came begging at her door for help.

"It's . . . different. Sort of," I admit. "Some of it feels the same. But it mostly feels like . . . a storm? One I've seen build before. And . . . I'm scared."

"Scared?"

I nod. "Of what it will do to me this time. Once it hits. What it will do to my family . . . and . . ."

"And?" she asks.

I swallow the lump in my throat. ". . . and what they will think of me if I'm not as strong."

36

"Ah." Iris sits back in her chair and tilts her head to the side as she looks at me. Her pale gray eyes are almost an exact match for the sheet of silver hair that falls in a perfect curtain to her shoulders. "Are you sure you are afraid of the event? Or are you afraid of if and how people will judge your response after it's happened?"

It's like getting hit with a bag of bricks right in the stomach. The wind is completely knocked out of me. And as much as it elicits a knee-jerk reaction from me, she's right. In a way, I am scared of what people will think of me. Will I overreact? Underreact? Will it seem performative of me to be heartbroken and shattered? And if I'm not, does that mean I'm cold and heartless? Is there even a perfect way to grieve someone?

"I guess, all of it?" My answer comes out as more of a question.

"Sometimes it's easier for us to focus on the superficial reactions rather than actually sitting in our emotions. It feels . . . safer. Would you agree?"

I nod, because yes, of course I agree. I have almost an entire life's worth of experience with that particular skill. It's always been easy for me to figure out what other people need, and like a chameleon, I've always been able to change my color to suit them. Unfortunately, that's what landed me here in the first place. Twenty-five years of not understanding your own emotions is not impressive. It's sad. I didn't even feel like a person anymore. I was just this husk that twisted and bent in every way possible until one day I snapped, and for the first time in years actually felt something: anger.

It wasn't my proudest moment, but after an entire weekend of being taken for granted and bossed around by my uncle who I was taking care of after his knee surgery, I lost it. I had barely slept in three days, setting alarms for medications, turning him in bed, helping him to the bathroom, all without even a small thank-you. Then, when I finally had some time to myself, I was going to take a shower when I heard his buzzer from down the hall. It usually meant he was hungry or wanted something to eat, so I said I needed just ten minutes and I would be there. It was the fastest shower of my life, and when I walked back into his room only seven minutes later, he was screaming some of the most severe obscenities that I had ever heard, along with several sentiments that continued to ring in my years ever since: selfish, undeserving, self-righteous, spoiled, heartless. All because I dared to take a seven-minute shower.

I accepted each verbal punch one punch after the other until I couldn't take anymore. Then, without saying a word, I walked over to his side table, grabbed the buzzer, and smashed it against the floor. I lost count of how many times I stomped on its broken plastic parts, but by the time I came back to reality, the majority of it was in bits not much bigger than a puzzle piece. We never spoke again, and he passed away a few months later after overdosing on opioids. I didn't attend his funeral. Maybe I should have forgiven him. One more thing to feel guilty about, I guess.

And now I'm here, sitting with Iris these long years later debating the same questions in different ways. Oh how the wheel keeps turning.

"What was the last thing you did that made you feel real joy, L?"

The question catches me off guard.

"Real joy?" I hear myself echoing her.

She nods her head, her silver blanket of hair bouncing near her shoulders in a mesmerizing wave.

"Pure joy," she elaborates. "Something that filled you and every corner of your being with light."

I look at her as if she has grown horns. Filled me with light? What on Earth is that supposed to mean? Do people really ever feel that way? Even half-filled with light seems like a distant dream made for books and movies: nice to think about, but impossible to obtain.

I shake my head. "Never?"

Iris sets down her notepad and pen on her desk and looks up at the clock.

"Our session is almost done, so I will leave you with this. Your homework is to come up with and check off as many things from a childish joy bucket list as you possibly can in the next six weeks."

"A bucket list for children? That seems a bit morbid."

Usually this is when people get fed up with me and let out a long, dramatic sigh. But to Iris' credit, all she does is give me a soft smile.

"Children aren't aware of some of the burdens of the world, so it is often easier for them to experience joy in whole doses. So, imagine you were a child right now, or even a teenager. Is there something that you would want to do, or something that you actually did want to do, that might have brought you peace or comfort or happiness that you could do now?" She looks at the clock again. "I'll let you think on it. Make a list, and see how many things you can cross off before we meet again."

I nod, still a bit unsteady thinking about how I could possibly hold joy when I am so used to juggling my demons. I am suddenly scared I won't have enough mental hands for the exercise. But, if Iris thinks it's a good idea, I trust her. She hasn't led me astray so far.

"Thanks, Iris," I say as I stand.

She stands with me to escort me to the back door. "Call me if you need another session before then, okay, L? And, as always, you are doing amazing work. Don't forget to give yourself some grace and acknowledgement for everything you've done. And if you haven't heard it in a while, I am proud of you."

I immediately don't know where to look. Heat from the embarrassment of the praise works its way up my face and settles in my cheeks.

"Oh, I haven't done much. It's not like—"

Iris' look cuts me off. We've discussed this: my inability to accept compliments, and the way I immediately knock myself down again. It's safer on the ground than on a pedestal.

"Thank you," I say instead, just like we practiced.

A genuine smile plays across her lips, showing a row of perfect white teeth, except for the one that would be a vampire fang if she was a monster, which is slightly tilted to the back of her mouth. She's not a monster, for the record. Far from it.

"Have a good day, L," is the last thing I hear from her before she gently shuts the door behind me with a soft click.

As I walk back to my car, all I can think of is how tired I already am just from imagining joy. How am I supposed to actually experience it? I've lived with my demons for so long, frankly it would be a miracle if they just disappeared and let me have a moment of peace. Walking through the darkness is safe, familiar. I know the feel of each shadow and stone of my mind. What if allowing in some light changes everything?

And worse, what if it doesn't?

7 | A | C | R | O | S | S

7 | | | | | | | |

Bars have alcohol. Alcohol is a solution. Therefore bars have

_ _ _ _ _ _ _ _.

September 30, 2024

"You should really just go," Mira says in between bites of her salad. This one has some kind of mushroom and egg in it. In the mason jar, it almost looks like she had been foraging in the forest and came out with a perfect blend of greens and other various goods. I briefly wonder if my friend is an elf. Or maybe a faerie? I finally settle on forest nymph. If I were to ever write a fantasy novel inspired by my friends, she would definitely be the whimsical, sweet, and upbeat creature living in the woods, who just happened to know everything about moss. Biology teacher was undoubtedly the right profession for her.

"He would want you to go. You know, to keep up your streak!" Jo adds.

"Yeah, you can't lose your place in the standings!"

Pops and I are almost last on the leaderboard, but I don't remind them of that. Our interests are far too niched to maintain a consistent score. Still, we haven't missed a trivia night at The Hawk for over five years. Except if you count that one time where there was a whole host of horses in front of the building that refused to move, which I don't. There was a farmer's market filled with carrots, apples, and just about everything else a horse would look for on their great escape. The Agriplex was only a few hundred meters away, and within a few hours, all of them had been rounded up and brought back to the stables. No one believes me when I tell them that story, but unless you've lived in a small town, you probably won't understand the completely bonkers shit that happens here on a day-to-day basis.

"It would be weird to go without him, plus I have exams to grade," I say in my defense. The truth is, I'm not sure my heart can take being there without him. Even though he's just a phone call or a two-hour drive away, it feels as if he's on the other side of the world.

"Stop making excuses, L." Vic always sees more than they let on. And unfortunately for me, today they seem to have X-ray vision that goes straight through the thoughts in my brain. "You can make up the extra hours tomorrow if you really need to."

They're right, of course, but I'm still hesitant.

"I don't have a partner." Another excuse.

Vic raises an eyebrow at me, but it's Mira that answers.

"It's just trivia, Do you really need one?"

Well no, but that's not the point.

"I've always been on a team of two." I shrug and take a sip of my coffee, which is basically my lifeline at this point.

"Well, I'm free tonight, so I can go with you," she says matter-of-factly.

Great. And now I'm out of reasons not to go now.

But could it really be that bad? If we're talking about our score, then yes. Mira's knowledge and mine overlap far too much to be any good at the games tonight. But, I did promise Iris I would search for small moments of joy if I can get them.

I reach down into my bag and pull out my day planner. Then, in the seven o'clock spot, I write *Trivia with Mira.*

Mira and I are the first to arrive. At least, I thought we were. That is until I look over at our table—yes, I know it's not technically our table since it belongs to a restaurant/jazz club, but Pops and I have been sitting there for five years, and okay, maybe I put our initials on the bottom of the table in permanent marker one night when I'd had too many London Lemonades, but that's not my fault. I still maintain that the fermented juniper berries and I were left unattended for far too long. And we don't need to talk about how I was twenty-eight years old at the time. Nope. Not talking about it—and see that there is someone sitting in my chair. No, not just someone. I recognize those dark curls and his earrings and . . . the lip ring.

Dear Universe,

> *You're fucking with me, right?*

Sincerely, L

Again, yes I know it's not my chair, but it's where I always sit on the last Monday of every month because it's trivia night. Plus, the chair is shaped like an L, so ha! It does have my name on it. Clearly infallible logic.

"L?" There's a hint of concern in Mira's voice, and that's when I realize I haven't moved since I saw him sitting in my seat at our table.

"Coming," I reply and follow her to the bar.

"Hey, L," Jerr greets me as we approach the bench. He looks behind me expectantly and my heart sinks, anticipating his next question. "Where's your old man?"

There it is.

"Running some tests in Calgary," I say, trying not to let the anxiety show through my voice.

Jerr nods in understanding as he takes out a champagne glass from below and prepares to make my drink. "Lougheed?" he asks.

I shake my head. "Foothills."

"Ah, well, hopefully they take good care of him and get him home soon."

I put on my best mask and give him a warm smile. "Thanks, Jerr. I'll pass that along."

As he pours the gin into the tall glass, loose strands of his soft gray hair bounce in front of his face. After he fills the rest with lemonade and places three ice cubes on top, he looks over to Mira. "And for you?"

She pinches her lips to the side slightly before looking over at my drink and ordering one for herself.

"Chicken fingers?" he asks me. He doesn't have to. Just like my drink, I always order the same thing. It's what we do. We share chicken fingers and then whatever cheesecake is on special that week.

I nod. "You know it."

I give him one of Pops' trademark winks for good measure. It always works for him.

Mira and I turn around with our drinks and inspect the nearly empty room.

"Where do you want to sit?"

The one place that's taken, I think to myself, and then blush because that sounds like I want to sit on Ashe's lap, which is definitely not the case.

Mira lets out a soft giggle as she follows my gaze. "Please don't tell me that's your spot."

In response, I don't say anything. I mean, she did say not to tell her.

She sighs, takes my arm, and starts us in the direction of the table.

I pull back, halting us for a moment. "No, it's okay, really. We'll just—"

"L, we've been friends a long time. And I know your signs. We'll just start with asking if he's waiting for anyone, okay?"

I nod, even though I kind of just want to get the chicken fingers to go and then re-watch *Lord of the Rings* for the hundredth time in the comfort of my own home instead of being the pest that comes off as a spoiled brat because their favorite chair in a restaurant is currently occupied. But exposure therapy to small conflicts is also on my homework list that I neglected last month, and this seems relatively small, right?

"Hi," Mira says, and I'm suddenly aware that we are at the table, standing directly in front of Ashe.

"Hi," he responds. His voice is low, but smooth, and even though I've only heard it a handful of times, it feels almost familiar.

"Are these seats taken?" she asks.

He shakes his head and gestures at the other chairs. "Be my guest."

I take Pops' chair, which is on the side of the square table closest to the door, and immediately to the left of Ashe. Mira sits to my left as well, which I hold my tongue about because she'll never be able to see the projector screen from there, unless somehow she has learned to turn her head all the way around like an owl.

"Fancy meeting you here," Ashe says, eyes on me.

I have been solely interacting with teenagers and my friends for so long that I have absolutely no idea how to do this "small talk" thing. Am I supposed to ask about his day? Make a compliment? Talk about the weather? Give a fun fact about the science of making gin?

"I bet you're thankful there isn't a door nearby," I say.

Smooth, the gremlins echo.

Ashe gives me a small smirk, and the skin pinches around his eyes slightly. "There's a first time for everything."

A group of people walk in and I twist around to see who it is. The three Lambley sisters, all dressed in matching pink "TRI-VI-YEAH!" shirts take their chairs at the table nearest to the screen. They all have bad vision. Each of their glasses are thick and make their eyes look like tiny pins on their faces. It's an unspoken agreement that their table has to be close, and something tells me that Jerr inches it up a little bit every time as well to help them out. They're the only team below me and Pops, but I've never seen them without smiles. Their booming laughs are nothing short of contagious, and I find myself grinning with them. I briefly wonder if these sixty-year-old women have found the secret to happiness, and make a mental note to ask them about it later.

"So, are you here for trivia night?" Mira asks Ashe.

He nods. "And you two?"

"Yeah, L usually comes with their pops, but I had to fill in tonight."

"Oh." A look of concern crosses Ashe's face, and here we are again with me having to answer questions about Pops. "Is everything okay?"

"Just some tests." I wave away his concern with my hand in front of my face.

Maybe if I say it enough times, it will wash away the ball of anxiety nestled in my gut as well. But something tells me that's just wishful thinking.

"Do you have a partner?" I ask, trying to change the subject.

"No, I've been single for a few months now."

I flush. "Oh, uhm, that's not—I mean—"

Ashe laughs. "Sorry, my misunderstanding. I'm used to people being direct and just assumed. No, I don't have a partner for trivia either."

Is that a hint of a blush on his cheeks as well? And why do I find it so . . . endearing?

"I'm sorry too, I'm usually more clear about things. Scientist and all."

Sure, make everything about you.

The gremlins really won't leave me alone today. Maybe I need to talk to my doctor about upping my dosage. Or maybe Iris is right and I'm just extremely overworked and overwhelmed.

"Chemistry, right?" he asks.

I nod. "Yes, and Mira teaches biology. It's fascinating trying to figure out how everything works together, you know?"

Ashe thinks about this for a second before responding.

"Not really," he admits. "I wasn't much of a science kid."

"Oh." I'm actually surprised. I can't remember a time I wasn't completely enthralled with the concept of science. Even when I was a toddler, I was always asking Mom how things worked. Eventually she just bought me books on everything from dinosaurs to constellations and bugs. I wasn't particularly fond of the creepy-crawlies, but I was completely obsessed with my first-ever baking set. The day that Mom taught me how to bake bread completely changed my life.

Learning how the yeast made everything rise from just a little bit of warm water and sugar was fascinating. After that, I was a goner. Head over heels for something I could never see with my eyes, only with my mind.

There's a short awkward silence that stretches between us before I realize that I should probably say something else to fill it.

"So, what kind of a kid were you?"

He chuckles and takes a sip of his beer. "Depends on who you ask," he says. "My aunts would probably say that I was an adorable chaos gremlin. And my nan . . ."

Ashe swallows and looks down at his pint glass. It's not quite three-quarters empty, but he stands up and tells us that he needs a refill.

Mira's phone beeps with the Kim Possible theme and it lights up on the table.

"Oh shit," she says after reading the message.

"Everything okay?"

She puts her phone back down and gives me an apologetic look.

"I was supposed to meet with my parents over FaceTime tonight to discuss Thanksgiving plans."

"Oh, it's okay. We can go. It's starting to get crowded in here anyway."

It's not a lie. Somehow in the last three minutes, The Hawk has had a Mary Shelley makeover and completely come back to life. Did I miss the lightning?

"If it's not too bold of me to say, I think you should stay."

"What?" The word drops out of my mouth before I have time to think it.

"Ashe seems nice and he doesn't have a trivia partner. Maybe you two can pair up."

I give her a skeptical look.

"I don't know, Mira. Maybe we should just call this a bust and take off."

"Take off?" Ashe says from behind me. "Did something happen?"

"Yes," Mira says before I have a chance to reply. "I am late for a date with my parents, and L here is going to be down a trivia partner, so it looks like we are all in luck with you in our company tonight, Ashe."

I barely say goodbye before she's given me a peck on the cheek and made her way out the door.

A few seconds later, I get a text from her:

Have fun. Experience joy. And if it's too much, I'm only a text away. You know the rules.

Xx

I sigh and put my phone away. I could go. But oddly enough there is a part of me that wants to stay. I want to know more about this man who sticks out in the crowd like a sore thumb, and makes me feel . . . less alone.

I decide to try. What harm could it do anyway?

"I know it's a weird question, but . . . can I have your chair?"

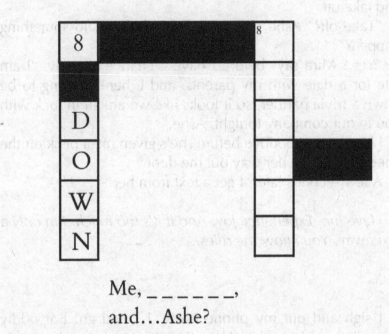

Me, _ _ _ _ _ _,
and...Ashe?

September 30, 2024

"What's up, Holmies? You could have been anywhere in the world right now, but you're here, at The Hawk! Who's ready for Trivia Night?"

Beau starts off every session this way: as if he's inviting us to a cabinet meeting in a Hamilton performance. The podium is far too short for him, but he still leans over onto his elbows with the microphone in hand while he scans the crowd. Seemingly satisfied, he nods his head and flicks his short, choppy brown hair out of his eyes as he points toward the screen behind him.

"Ladies and gentlemen, queers and peers, here is our list of categories for the evening!"

Beau flicks his wrist in the air as if performing some kind of magic to turn the projector on. We all know he has the remote in his other hand, but we still let out a chorus of *ahhhs* as the "magic" works, revealing the familiar five-by-five block of squares. The names of each column sit at the top. Today's topics are: The Very Best, Home on the Range, Life in the Fast Lane, Blast from the Past, and How It's Made.

"Any idea what they mean?" Ashe asks me.

I shrug. "Could be anything from musicals to space memes. You never know with Beau."

Jerr brings me my chicken fingers with extra ketchup as the Lambley sisters pick their category to get the night started.

"Anything else for you folks?" he asks.

I shake my head. "Not unless you have some insider knowledge on the game?"

He gives me a disapproving look.

"Worth a shot. Thanks, Jerr."

There's a long silence across the room, and then, to my surprise, Ashe raises his hand.

"Yes, you in the back!" Beau calls, pointing to our table.

"Is it Namakura Gatana?"

"Nama-what?" I find myself saying.

"Namakura Gatana, the oldest anime, right?"

"Correct! Two hundred points to . . ."

"Ashe." He turns to look at me and asks softly, "We are partners, right?"

I'm still trying to figure out how he could have possibly known about the anime, so I just stare at him blankly and give him a small nod as I chew.

"And L," he finishes.

"Great! Two hundred points to Ashe and L! We'll add that to your total tally."

Beau leans over to a screen on the podium and punches in our names and score, which then flash behind him on the leaderboard.

"L, since y'all are next up on our list, it's your turn to pick a category."

I'll probably have the best luck with the last topic, so I choose How It's Made for four hundred.

The question pops up and Beau reads it out loud.

"Erectile tissue is present in many different parts of the body, but surprisingly not in this area."

I laugh and wipe my face with my napkin before answering. If Mira had stayed, she would have been all over this one too. It is her favorite fun fact, after all.

"The nipples."

"Correct! Four hundred points to Ashe and L."

I reach over to my drink and catch Ashe's eyes on me. His face is lit up with amusement and . . . pride?

"How did you know that?" he asks me.

"Mira. She loves to tell us her daily facts from her calendar. This one was from last October I think? For Breast Cancer Awareness Month? There were a lot of boob facts. That one was memorable, because we had an extensive conversation about 'eargasms' afterward."

His brows knit together. "Eargasms?"

I nod. "You know, like when you're cleaning your ears or if you're getting a face massage and they start working their way around your lobes and it's like you're transported to a different realm?"

I roll my eyes back in my head for good measure.

"Can't say I've ever had an ear massage," he says.

"It's life-changing, you should really try it sometime."

"I might have to take you up on that."

I choke on my drink and let out a series of loud coughs. Did he really just—

"Are you okay?"

I wave away his concern with my hand, and Beau calls on us.

"Ashe and L!"

What? Oh shit, he thinks we have an answer.

My eyes are watering from the liquid stuck in my throat. I can't make out the words on the screen, let alone answer the question.

"*Death Note*. And Jerr was it?" Ashe asks. "Can we have some water here please?"

I regain my ability to see and breathe before Jerr makes it over, but I'm still thankful for the water when it arrives.

"What's a death note?" I finally manage to ask.

Ashe looks at me as if I have grown a second head or a third eye. Have I? I check my forehead for good measure.

"Your name is L."

I meet his stare, equally as confused as he appears to be.

"Yes? I think we've already established that."

He shakes his head. "No, your name is L . . . and you've never seen *Death Note*?"

"Oh, it's a movie?" I ask.

Ashe blinks a few times and raises his eyebrows. "I"—he scans me from head to toe as if looking for something—"you're fucking with me, right?"

Do I have food on myself?

I check my chest before returning his gaze. "What?"

"Your leg. How you're sitting."

He gestures to my knee, which is pointing up toward the ceiling. My foot is tucked close to my butt on the chair. It's how I always sit. Well, how I always sit now. Mom used to get on my case when I was younger, but it's been years since someone pointed it out.

Do I have a hole in my pants?

I look over the stretched fabric but come up empty. "What's wrong with it?"

Ashe lets out a low chuckle and runs his hand through his hair.

"Nothing, L." He pauses for a moment, and something in his look changes. "But if I need to learn about ear massages and erectile tissue, then you need to watch the best anime of all time."

Despite everything, I laugh. A true, genuine, real laugh. And I'll be damned, but it feels . . . good.

A wide smile works its way across Ashe's face. "What?"

It takes me a few moments to compose myself again.

"It's just . . . you're not what I expected."

"Oh?" He raises his eyebrow at me again.

"In a good way," I add. "I just thought that maybe you'd be . . . I don't know . . . a little more rough around the edges? Really into heavy metal? Maybe a cult member?"

It's Ashe's turn to laugh now.

"Well, I do love my Scandinavian metal. And I only attend cult events on Wednesday evenings, so you're safe tonight."

"Oh good. No danger of being sacrificed then?" I tease back.

"Well, I didn't say that." He smirks.

I reach over to take the salt shaker from the middle of the table and hold it over my neck, sprinkling a few crystals onto my skin.

I barely recognize who this person is. Is this what fun feels like?

"Well, do your gods like them seasoned?"

Something flashes behind Ashe's eyes that leaves my mouth feeling dry. Blood rushes to my face.

Did I take this too far?

There's a brief moment of hesitation before he sits back in his seat and shakes his head at me. "You know, if you wanted to do tequila shots, all you had to do was ask."

My face burns from embarrassment. Yup. Definitely too far.

"That's probably not the best idea," I admit, setting the salt down again. Mira and I had a bit too much fun celebrating her birthday last year. I'm still not sure my liver has fully recovered.

A look of amusement settles across his face. "Yeah, I've had a few of those experiences too," he says as if reading my mind.

"Ashe and L, it's your turn again," Beau says from the small stage.

All of the two-hundred-point spaces have been taken. I probably have the best luck staying with How It's Made, but Ashe seems to have luck with the Blast from the Past and The Very Best . . . But since I'm not much of a gambler, I decide to stay where I'm comfortable.

"How It's Made for six hundred please, Beau."

The question pops up on the screen.

"This part of the uterine reproductive system is not physically connected to it."

I work through the diagram in my mind. The uterus, the fallopian tubes, and the—

"The ovaries," I say proudly.

"Really?" Ashe asks from beside me.

"Yup! There are these teeny tiny hairs at the end of the fallopian tube called cilia that kind of sweep the fluid in the area toward the opening. Then, when the egg has been released from the ovary, it gets kind of caught up in the current and enters the fallopian tube."

I love sharing little tidbits of information about anything science- or space-related. At first, I'm filled with a brief sense of . . . joy? Is that what this is? This warmth of pure sunshine growing in my chest? Then I remember that most people outside of my friends and family don't really care for random side notes like that, which drags me right back down. If Ashe didn't think I was a bit off my rocker before, he definitely will now.

"That's . . . actually really weird and cool?"

I glance up and meet his eyes, which are wide and bright. To my surprise, he seems genuinely interested.

I let myself relax as much as I can.

"It is," I agree. "Humans are very strange creatures, but it's always interesting to piece them apart, you know?"

Ashe gives me a wry grin. "Maybe I should be the one who's worried about being sacrificed, Dr. Lecter."

My jaw drops as I realize what I've just said. "No—that's not what—I mean, I don't—"

He starts laughing, and those lines at the sides of his face come back. I hadn't noticed before, but he has two dimples: one on each cheek. His boyish enjoyment makes me begin to chuckle as well.

"You're ruthless," I say, giving him a playful elbow.

"Hey, don't be so quick to judge." Ashe holds his hands up as if in mock surrender. "I'm not the one playing cannibal over here."

I nudge him again and say the only thing that could possibly make it worse. I'm so far in, why back out now?

"It's okay, Ashe, eat your heart out."

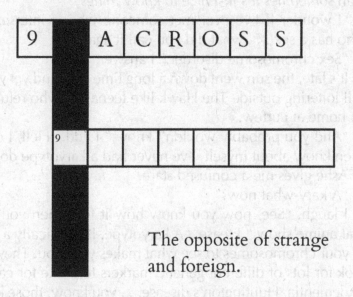

| 9 | | A | C | R | O | S | S |

The opposite of strange
and foreign.

September 30, 2024

By the end of the night, we moved up three places on the leaderboard. Not only that, but I successfully delivered three separate lectures on echidna penises, how the use of cardinal directions in space makes no sense (looking at you, *Star Wars*), and my personal favorite: how there are over half a dozen human sex chromosome combinations which can lead to a variety of secondary sex characteristics.

Even though Ashe never showed any hint of being annoyed or overwhelmed with my rambling, there was, and still is, a part of me that is incredibly self-conscious of taking up unnecessary space in conversation. The mind gremlins always have a thing or two to say about how no one will ever actually use this information, so why is it worth saying? And to be honest, I've never found a satisfactory rebuttal other than *sometimes it's just nice to know things.*

"I wonder if I've ever met someone who is intersex, or who has a sex . . . what did you call it again?"

"Sex chromosome disorder," I answer.

It's late, the sun went down a long time ago, and yet we're still loitering outside The Hawk like teenagers who refuse to go home at curfew.

"And you probably wouldn't know," I add. "Hell, I don't even know about myself. I've never had a karyotype done."

Ashe gives me a confused stare.

"A kary-what now?"

I laugh. "See, now you know how it felt when you said that anime show," I tease. "A karyotype. It's basically a map of your chromosomes to see what makes you, you. They can look for lots of different genetic markers too, like for cancer or dementia, Huntington's disease. . . you know, those kinds of things."

And I'm rambling again . . . great.

I pull my coat up around my neck. The wind has picked up, and the cool autumn air sends a shiver down my spine. Ashe leans against the brick siding and braces his foot against the wall and the cement walkway in front of the restaurant. He closes his eyes and takes a long, deep breath. When he lets it go, silver swirls form in the night in front of him, illuminated by the neighboring streetlamp. I guess Ashe has finally reached his tipping point, and since we're no longer in public, he doesn't have to put on a performance anymore. My heart sinks.

"Sorry," I say softly. It's basically a reflex at this point.

He tilts his head to the side and slowly opens his eyes at me. "Why did you stop?"

Something turns in my chest. "W—what?"

He completely turns to face me, his shoulder now the only point of contact against the wall. "You stopped . . . Why?"

I curl my toes in my shoes. I could lie and say I didn't have anything else to say, but for some reason, I don't want to be that way with him. There's a chance for me to be *me*, here and now, and it's fucking terrifying, but . . . he's basically a stranger. What could I possibly lose if I took off my mask for a second?

"It's just . . . people don't like listening to me, and—"

"I do," he interrupts. Ashe pushes himself off the wall and closes the space between us. The streetlamp behind him outlines his silhouette in a soft white that makes him look like something from out of this world.

"But you . . . just now. The exasperated sigh?"

Ashe's lips pinch to the side and he gives me a low laugh that seems to come straight from his chest.

"I'm sorry," he breathes. He's only an arm's length away from me now, but I swear I can feel his heat from here. All of the ice in the air seems to have completely evaporated around us. "I was . . . overwhelmed." His voice shakes just slightly at the end. "It was a lot of new people to be around. I just . . . needed a second."

Oh. Of course. I didn't even consider how tonight would have been for him. Someone new entering a space full of people who have known each other for years or even decades. To be bombarded with new sounds, new faces, new questions, new spaces. Suddenly, I feel horrible for assuming that he was fake, disinterested, and judgemental. He's just human. And sometimes humans need a fucking break. The Universe knows I do.

"No, I'm sorry," I start, holding my hands up slightly in front of me. "I shouldn't have assumed—"

"So it's to be a Canadian standoff now, is it?" The teasing tone is back in his voice and he smirks at me. "It's okay, L. Tell me about the karyotypes."

A ball of warmth floods my stomach and makes its way up to my cheeks.

"Really?" I feel like a child who has just been allowed to take a new toy home for the first time.

Ashe nods and sits on the walkway. He taps the spot beside him, and I follow to take the place at his side. "I insist," he says.

I grab a small rock from in front of me and roll it over in my hand. "Did you know that it's possible to have two X chromosomes and still grow testes? That's what I mean—how unless you have a karyotype done, you don't know for certain what kind of chromosomal makeup you have."

Ashe takes a rock of his own and twists it around his fingers. "I didn't know that," he admits. "How does that work though?"

"Not a lot of people do, but it's possible for the SRY gene to be on an X chromosome. It's a small genetic mistake that can have very real consequences. But it is possible, and it does exist."

He nods and gives me a playful nudge with his shoulder. "And here I was thinking that you were just a chemistry nerd," he teases.

I roll my eyes. "Well, not just." I laugh. "I technically have three undergrad degrees—in chemistry, biochemistry, and education. But since biochemistry isn't really an option to teach in high school, I chose chemistry. Mira is a lot better at teaching in the bio department anyway."

"I don't know," Ashe says. "I've learned a lot tonight."

"Well, you're not like other folks." The words come out of my mouth before I give them complete permission, and I bite my lip, worried he might take it the wrong way. "I mean, you're not a teenager with better things to do than listen to me go on about science all day and night."

He lets out a soft sigh and turns the rock over again, rubbing his thumb along the smooth surface.

"They're lucky to have you."

I'm just about to comment on how I would love to have that in writing so I can look at it on the hard days, when he stands up and offers me a hand.

I take it, and when our skin touches, it doesn't make me feel like I have to recoil. To my surprise, I'm not uncomfortable with the contact.

"How about that *Death Note* promise?" Ashe asks.

There it is.

It feels like a punch to the chest, knocking the wind out of me. The edges of my vision go slightly blurry and there's a high-pitched ringing in my ears. Whatever peace I felt in that moment is completely gone, replaced by an insatiable fear eating away at the small streaks of light that had peeked through the cracks in my mind.

I take my hand away as slowly and inconspicuously as possible. Now the skin on my hand is on fire, sending hot tendrils of sparks and flames up my arm, straight through my neck and up into my brain. Is he . . . asking me back to his place? What if he tries to kiss me? Or more? I mean, not that it's a bad thing, but with someone I just met?

Don't be so self-obsessed.

"Actually, I should probably go home. I have a lot of marking to do."

Not a lie, but not exactly the truth either.

Remarkably, Ashe doesn't look concerned or taken aback.

"No problem. In case you change your mind, or want to take me up on it another time, can I give you my number?"

"Oh, uhm, yeah, sure."

I pull out my phone from my back pocket, open it up to my contacts, and give it to him.

He types a few things in and hands it back to me, still on the contact screen, as if giving me one last chance to formally accept it.

"Thanks for tonight, L," he says. "It was really nice to meet you. Properly, I mean."

I smile and nod back. "It was nice to make a new friend," I tell him, and I find that I actually mean it.

"Have a good night, L. See you tomorrow."

"Just steer clear of any doors," I call after him as he makes his way to his vehicle.

"I'll do my best to stay vigilant."

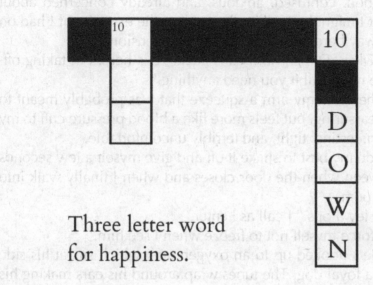

Three letter word
for happiness.

October 5, 2024

"He's all settled if you want to come over," Mom says through the phone.

It takes only a few minutes before I'm at Pops' apartment door holding a plate of fresh, and most importantly, still-warm cookies. Mom answers the door.

"He's in the living room," she says, holding the door open for me. Before I make it around her, she stops me with her hand on my elbow.

I look down at her hand and then back up into her eyes. She looks almost sad, but it could be mistaken for exhaustion. They always look the same on her. It's the line between her brows that gives it away. My throat goes dry. Did I miss something?

"Just . . . don't be worried or upset, okay?"

I nod, confused, anxious, and already concerned about what I might be walking into. All of the excitement I had on the way here melts away into apprehension.

"Okay, Dad," Mom calls back. "L is here. I'm taking off. Give me a call if you need anything."

She gives my arm a squeeze that was probably meant to be reassuring, but feels more like a blood pressure cuff to my brain: testing, tight, and terribly uncomfortable.

I do my best to shake it off and give myself a few seconds between when the door closes and when I finally walk into the room.

"Hey, Pops," I call as I enter.

I force myself not to freeze when I see him.

He's hooked up to an oxygen tank which sits at his side like a loyal dog. The tubes wrap around his ears making his sky-blue eyes look sunken and dull. It's not just the tubes though, it's also his skin, which is significantly paler than when I saw him in the hospital. It has taken on almost a gray tint, which reminds me of how Grams looked before . . .

No. I cast out the thought before it has the chance to properly form.

"Well, aren't you a sight for sore eyes," I try to tease, but somehow my tone comes out much flatter than I intended.

If Pops notices, he doesn't say anything.

"Oh, I know," he says, gesturing to himself. "Who wouldn't want a piece of this?"

He gives me a playful wink. "Unless of course, you're a vegetarian."

"Pops!"

The twinkle in his eyes returns as he laughs and reaches out to the plate in my hands.

"Are those what I think they are?"

"Your favorite," I say. "Moooooonster cookies," I snarl, trying to re-enact how I used to say it when I was a kid. For emphasis, I wrinkle my nose and pull my lips up as if exposing fangs.

"So ferocious, kid, as always."

I place the plate down on the side table and take a seat in the chair opposite him.

"So," Pops says, mouth full of cookies, "what did I miss?"

I fill him in on the last few days, my thoughts about how I can better help my students, how Charlie is running, how no one has won the Elusive Echo yet, and about Nyx and Nox.

Pops lets his cookie fall back into his hand, and he looks at me wide-eyed.

"What?" I ask, suddenly scared he's choking or something.

Oh fuck, have I just killed my grandfather?

"We missed trivia night!" he exclaims.

I sit back in my chair and take a deep breath. Jeez, if this man doesn't have a heart attack, I definitely will, at this rate.

"Well, kind of," I admit.

He raises a brow at me.

"I didn't want to break our streak," I say, "so Mira agreed to go with me."

He smiles at that. "I always did like that girl." He takes another bite. "So, did we win anything?" he asks.

"Well . . . we did move up a few places."

I bite my lip. Why am I so nervous to tell him about Ashe?

"Huh," he says. "All science questions?"

"No, not . . . all," I reply.

He narrows his eyes at me and leans forward. "I have known you your whole life, kid. I know when you're keeping something from me. So . . . what is it?"

I sigh and lean my head against the back of the chair, staring up at the ceiling.

"I . . . made a friend?"

"Is that a question I'm supposed to answer?"

"No? I don't know." I say quickly. "We met at the school. Actually, you'd probably get a kick out of how I hit him with my car."

"You ran someone over?" Pops exclaims.

"No, no! Just with my car door," I clarify. "And, I mean, he didn't run away screaming, so that's probably a good sign, right?"

Pops shrugs. "There are worse things."

"Anyway," I continue, "his name is Ashe, and well, he was at The Hawk. He was sitting at our table—"

"A crime," Pops interrupts.

I love this man.

"Agreed. So obviously Mira had to walk us right over—"

"And obviously you didn't want to confront him about it."

He knows me so well.

"Right, well, we get over there, and Mira gets a call saying she has to go, so Ashe and I ended up being partners. He was actually really good, and surprisingly easy to talk to. He wanted to watch a show after, but there's just so much going on, and I'm swamped with work, so I said no. And that's everything, I promise."

Pops gives me a disapproving look. The tubes that wrap around his ears only enhance his scowl.

"I'm sorry," I tell him. "I know it's our tradition and that we always do Trivia Night together, but Ashe didn't have a partner, and Mira had other family matters to attend to."

In less than a blink of an eye, the downward tilt of his lips flips up into a wide smile, and his infectious laugh echoes through the room.

"You think I'm upset because you went to The Hawk without me?" His laugh continues until it eventually evolves into a wet cough. This goes on for several almost concerning seconds before he catches his breath and continues. "L, I'm upset because you're making the same mistakes I did at your age, and you don't have to."

Confusion and surprise wash through my mind. The look on my face must be obvious because Pops goes on to fill in the gaps.

"When I met your grandmother, I was already engaged," he says.

I nod, because I've heard this story a hundred times. "I know."

He shakes his head. "No, you don't understand, L. I almost went through with the wedding. I was just going through the motions, doing what was expected of me. Doing what I expected of myself. Except . . . I woke up one morning and thought—"

"What does my life look like in five years? Ten years? Twenty? And I couldn't envision it without her by my side." I give him my best impression of his words that I heard at every anniversary and every birthday. "I know, Pops. You and Grams had a love story worthy of a romance novel. But that's not what this is. I've only properly talked with Ashe once, and I don't even really know him. Plus, I wasn't lying. I do have a lot of work to do. And it's not like I said no to a date—he was just asking about some anime."

Pops' stare dares to burn a hole through my head.

"Look, I'm not saying you have to marry the guy! I'm just saying that sometimes it's nice to get to know someone from scratch." He arches a bushy gray eyebrow at me. "L, maybe this is a chance to be yourself in a new way. Go explore. Have some fun. Make a new friend. Who knows? You might just learn something about yourself as well."

"You approve of someone you haven't even met?" I challenge.

Pops rotates himself in his chair so he can look at me more directly.

"I approve of you and your happiness. I might be an old man in a chair, but I'm not blind. You like him, and no, before you object, I don't mean romantically, although, for the record I'd probably be fine with that too, as long as you bring him over for a crossword someday." He clears his throat. "You like him, and that's okay, L. That's enough for me. Please let it be enough for you too."

Wise, as always.

"Are you trying to Gandalf me?"

He smirks. "Why? Is it working?"

I roll my eyes and bring out a folded piece of paper from my sweater. "Speaking of crosswords," I say as I smooth it out between us.

"I see what you're doing. But I'll let it go. Just this once." He takes out a pen from his shirt pocket and wags the end of it at me as he talks.

We spend the rest of our visit working through my home-made cookies and crossword prompts. Every once in a while, I have to give him an extra hint, but for the most part, he's able to fill in the blanks on his own. Finally, he lets out a long yawn. His stomach grumbles, but it's not from hunger, since he clearly had his share of sweets.

"Well, I hate to be the pooper of this party, but I think it might be time to take my job literally. Time to shit and sleep. Hopefully in that order."

"Polite as always," I say as I help him to his feet. "Thanks for the visit, Pops."

I wrap my arms around him, and he gives me a tight squeeze back.

There are still a few cookies left, so I leave them. I can come pick up the plate later anyway. Pops walks me to the door and I give him one more hug before leaving.

"Love you," I say as I turn around to wave goodbye.

"Have fun watching cartoons with your new boyfriend. Love you, kid. Toodles!"

"He's not my—"

He closes the door before I can finish. Pops always has to have the last word.

I sigh and walk back down the narrow corridor toward the reception desk.

What if he's right?

I can almost see Iris with her arms folded across her chest saying, *I told you so*. Pops' words echo hers in my mind. Am I happy spending time with Ashe? I don't know. It was only that one time. But it was fun, I guess.

I bring out my phone and hover over the message button.

Am I really doing this?

What's the worst that could happen?

I shake my head and type out a few words on the screen. When I read over them, they sound whiny and desperate so I delete them and try again. And again. And again. And again.

Finally, I just say "hi, this is L." I can figure out the rest after. Maybe. Probably not, but that's future L's problem.

I swallow down my nerves, close my eyes, and press send.

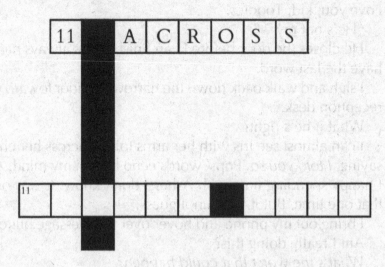

| 11 | | A | C | R | O | S | S |

| 11 | | | | | | | | | |

A series of experiences one might
enjoy before an untimely departure.

October 5, 2024

There are three knocks at the door. Nyx trots up beside me as I make my way over. I lean down and give her a few pats on her head. She pushes herself up into my palm like she always does. Nyx probably thinks it's Mom or Dad, or one of my friends.

I frown. She's never been particularly fond of strangers. Or other animals, for that matter, although she's fine with her sister, Nox. She's about as independent as it gets, and only accepts you once you've passed some kind of arbitrary test she has designed. I have yet to figure out what the parameters are of said trial, but that's probably for the best. Maybe humans aren't meant to understand cat logic.

After a slight nudge with my slippers, Nyx makes her way back to the living room. I open the door to find Ashe carrying two fabric grocery bags filled with . . . snacks?

"What are those?" I ask him.

Sure, interrogate the poor man instead of inviting him in. Who do you think he is? A vampire?

I mentally roll my eyes at the gremlins and motion for Ashe to come into the house. Can't hurt not to say the words. He crosses the barrier of the doorway with ease. Why do I find myself breathing a small sigh of relief? Vampires don't exist. But apparently my mind knows no bounds. Maybe the cat logic isn't the only thing that's completely unintelligible in this house.

"I'm sorry," he says as he places the bag on the island counter. "Nasty habit from my nan. She said that I should never go to anyone's house empty-handed and, well . . . I got a little carried away."

He slowly brings out three stacked containers and puts them beside the bag. "I hope you don't mind."

I shake my head. "Not at all, as long as you don't feed them to the cats."

"Oh, I wouldn't dare think of sharing these. Except with you, of course."

I give him a nod of appreciation in return.

"I have marshmallow squares, snickerdoodles, and everything to make crostinis."

"Wow," I say, gawking at the display. "You're a baker?"

He shrugs. "In a past life."

Nox gives a loud trill and trots up to us before rubbing against Ashe's leg.

"And who is this cute little shadow?"

"This is Nox. Be careful—she *will* roll over and trap you with her cute fluffy belly."

"As she should." Ashe laughs as he leans down to give her a few scratches between her ears.

"Her sister, Nyx, is around here somewhere too. She's not big into people though, so don't feel offended if she keeps her space."

"Oh, I promise to take it very personally," he replies.

"I'm sure she would love to hear that," I tease.

I turn and gesture to the adjoined kitchen and living room.

"Well, welcome to my humble abode. This is obviously the kitchen and the living room, and just down the hall over there is the bathroom, if you need it. And, uh, well, make yourself at home, I guess."

Ashe unzips his jacket and places it on the back of one of the barstools.

"Can I get you anything to drink? Water? Iced tea? Milk? Something stronger?"

"Water's fine," he says as he assembles the containers in his arms and brings them over to the coffee table. "Thank you."

I pour a glass for each of us and follow him into the living room.

"Do you have a preferred seat here as well?" he asks. There's a slight hint of teasing in his voice that I might not have picked up on had I not been so well versed in it thanks to my Pops.

I roll my eyes, thinking back to that horribly uncomfortable moment at The Hawk.

"Actually, yes, I do. I sit on the left side of the couch."

"Right side it is."

Before he takes his seat, he goes back to his bags and retrieves a few DVDs.

"I'm assuming you have something to watch these on?"

"Yup." I gesture to the small black box under the television.

"Old school," he says, nodding his head. "I like it."

"Yeah, well, I'm not a gamer and I can't afford to pay extra for streaming services, so DVD player it is."

He pops the first disc in and leaves the others on the coffee table.

"So," I say as I put the legs up on my side of the couch. "Anything I should know before starting this?"

Starting what? my gremlins say, wryly.

Okay, it's time to fuck off now, I counter.

"Not really," Ashe says as he sits back and goes to the settings on the main menu. "Captions?"

I nod. "Yes, please."

"Alright then." Ashe points the remote at the TV and presses play. "Welcome to *Death Note*."

Four hours later, I'm sitting with my feet under me, eyes glued on the television and absentmindedly gnawing on what is probably my hundredth snickerdoodle. Seriously, what did Ashe put in these?

"Well?" he asks as the credits play and he stands to change the disc again.

"I have so many questions," I admit. "Who is L? Where did he come from? Why is he literally so good at everything he does? Is he like Sherlock Holmes? Or did he go to school to be like this? Or both? And why do I want him and Light to fall in love and take over the world together?"

Ashe laughs, and it's one of the purest sounds I've ever heard. It makes me laugh in return.

"What?" I ask.

He shakes his head. A strand of hair has come loose from his bun and it twists in the air as he moves.

"Nothing. I just have never heard someone else want them to end up together as much as I do, is all."

I can't imagine how someone could not want these two to steal each other away.

"It's because of the enem—"

"ies to lovers trope . . ."

Ashe looks back and fixes his gaze on mine. A knowing smile stretches across his face.

"I knew you were a book nerd!" he says excitedly, pointing at me.

"And who knew *you* would be?"

He raises a shoulder and pinches his lips together nonchalantly. "I dabble," he admits.

I cross my arms over my chest. "You know what a book trope is, and you called me a book nerd. I say you do more than just dabble."

He raises his hands up as if in mock surrender. "Okay, fine. You got me there."

He sits back on the couch and faces me. "Favorite trope?" he asks.

I think about this for a second. I enjoy all kinds of books for all kinds of reasons. It's hard to narrow things down to just one unifying thing.

"Maybe 'Wise Old Mentor'? I don't know. It always reminds me of my Pops."

Ashe nods. "That's a good one."

"You?" I ask.

Am I mistaken or does a light pink dust his cheeks?

"Promise not to make fun of me?"

I furrow my brows. "Why would I make fun of you?"

He hesitates and bites the inside of his lip.

"Because it's a romance trope?"

I sit in silence, waiting for him to continue.

"It's . . . roommates-to-lovers."

Ashe squints at me, his honey-brown eyes tentatively peering through his long dark lashes.

"Oh good. I thought you were going to say insta-love," I tease. "Not that there's anything wrong with the trope—I just don't experience life that way, so I can't relate to it."

Ashe gives me a nervous giggle in response. "Me either," he admits. "Although there's something freeing in reading books about it, in my opinion."

I raise a brow at him, and he shrugs.

"What can I say? I'm a hopeless romantic. Just because I can't fall like that doesn't mean I can't appreciate it when others do. Imagine just being able to have a spark like that out of nowhere? Think of the excitement and wonder and possibilities you could look forward to every day. You'd wake up and think 'maybe today is the day that I run into them.'"

"Seems like an impossible dream for me," I say. "Can't relate."

"Me either," he agrees. "The universe speaks in riddles to us."

"Indeed. It's like one giant crossword puzzle of over-analyzing and self-evaluating."

"And some of us are better at taking hints than others."

I laugh. "Don't I know it."

The alarm goes off on my phone, signaling to me that it's time to take my medication.

"Sorry," I say, and turn it off. "One second."

I make my way into the kitchen, take out my beloved Lexapro, and swallow the pills down. Another day where I have won against my gremlins.

When I turn around, my eyes catch on the list I had started hanging on the fridge. There are only a few scribbled words, and I'd be lying if I said I was brave enough to start this journey on my own. My gaze wanders to Ashe, who is still comfortably resting on the couch, one hand behind his head, the fingers of the other tapping a gentle rhythm on his leg.

A thought occurs to me. Maybe it's impulsive, but if I don't ask now, I may never have the courage to ask again. Not only that, but without an extra push, I might not even follow through with this in the first place. And I wouldn't want to disappoint Iris. Would it hurt to ask? It's a risk, sure, but he doesn't really know me. He's just a stranger. A nice stranger, albeit, but a stranger nonetheless. Ashe's rejection or judgment would undoubtedly hurt less than anyone else's. New person. New experiences. New me. A chance to reinvent myself, or at the very least settle into myself. He doesn't know me, and some days I don't either. Pops' words echo in my mind. Could this be a chance . . . What do I have to lose?

"Ashe," I say as I come around the corner. I hold the paper in my hand, take a breath and ask before I have a chance to back out. "Have you ever heard of a childhood bucket list?"

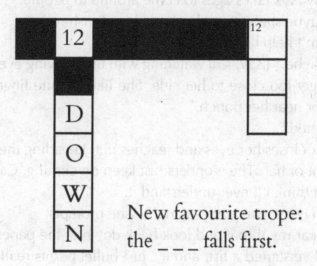

New favourite trope:
the _ _ _ falls first.

October 5, 2024

Nyx jumps up on the couch and looks at Ashe. That's usually her spot to sleep in the evening, and like me, we don't particularly enjoy being out of routine.

Without hesitation, Ashe reaches out and begins to scratch between her ears. To my surprise, she lets him. There's no growling. No hissing. She doesn't even pull back. If anything, she leans into his touch even more. Then, after a few seconds, she takes three small steps forward and nuzzles at his side.

I stare at him wide-eyed and mouth agape.

"What?" he asks.

"She . . . Nyx, I mean. She never does that."

Ashe looks down at her, confused. "But didn't she come up when we were at the counter earlier?"

I shake my head. "No, that was Nox. She's a lot friendlier. Usually Nyx takes ages to come around to people."

"Maybe she's found her insta-love," Ashe teases.

I can't help but laugh.

"Maybe," I say, still watching with unbelieving eyes. "Just don't get too close to her side. She likes to bite fingers that wander near her pouch."

"Noted."

Nyx closes her eyes and reaches out, kneading the couch in front of her. The wonders just keep on coming. Cat logic. I don't think I'll ever understand it.

"Anyway, you were saying?" Ashe prompts.

I clear my throat and look back down at the paper. "Yes, well, I've started a list, and it's just bullet points really, but I think it could be . . . fun?"

Ashe tilts his head at me. "Not the best sales pitch," he says.

I pinch my lips to the side. "Well then I guess it's a good thing I'm not a sales person trying to swindle you."

He shrugs. "Fair point." He thinks for a moment. "Okay, I'm in."

I blink a few times. "That's it?"

"Sure," he says, still petting Nyx. "Why not? I think we could all use a little extra joy these days and . . . "

"And?"

He gives me a tilted smile. "Spending time with you is . . . fun?"

I roll my eyes. "Is that a question?"

Ashe looks back down at Nyx and begins to rub under her chin. She lifts it up appreciatively.

"You tell me," he says.

My eyes are getting quite the workout today. "Okay, fine, yes, it's fun."

I sit back down on the couch.

The words catch at the back of my throat. I want to tell him that I think it's more than just about superficial fun. I feel safe enough to take a full breath around him. That sometimes you just click with people, and it's impossible to explain, and I'm so Universe-damned terrible at this making friends thing and I don't even know where to start. Clearly a paradigm-shifting philosophical exercise in experiencing joy as an adult was the best option to open this door.

I give him the paper and he takes it with his other hand so he can keep petting Nyx. Perks of being a cat, I guess.

Ashe carefully reads the scratched words on the page.

"Stay up all night reading? Twist my rubber arm."

I let out a giggle at his words.

"I figured you might be interested in that one."

He gives me a confused look. "What's tub painting?"

"What it sounds like, I guess," I say. "You sit in the tub and paint, and then when you're done, you wash it off and call it a day. No rules, no guidelines, just permission to be messy and chaotic."

Ashe nods. "Okay then," he says as he hands the paper back to me.

"Is there anything you'd want to do?" I ask. "I mean, if you're going to be a part of this experiment, you might as well be an agent in it."

Ashe looks up to the ceiling. "An agent, you say?"

"Well, I mean—"

"Can we do laser tag then?"

I pause for a moment. "Laser tag?"

"Sure, why not? There's fewer things more joyful than getting your ass kicked by a bunch of kids at an entertainment arcade."

I am not convinced. "Not quite my idea of fun, but I guess we could try?"

"I mean, there's always YouTube dance lessons as well."

I wince. "I think I'd prefer the embarrassment of losing to children over the embarrassment of my two left feet."

He shrugs. "Suit yourself."

"Anything else?" I ask.

Ashe's teeth graze his lower lip and his eyes drop to the floor.

"What is it?"

He takes a few breaths before answering. "Is there a place to . . . see the stars?"

"See the stars? Like an observatory?"

He shakes his head. "No, like just to look at them. I could never see them clearly in the city."

I scratch stargazing down on the list.

"We don't really need a specific place for that," I say. "Just drive a few minutes out of town and that should do it."

Ashe's eyes light up at my words.

I make an extra note to remember my book of constellations as well.

"You're really okay doing these things too? It is your experiment, after all."

I nod. "I love going for drives along the back roads, and as for laser tag . . . well, I guess that remains to be seen," I tease.

Ashe yawns and stretches.

"Well, now that we have that settled, I think I might have to call it a night. Any idea on when you might want to get started on this list of yours?"

I look over at my calendar on the fridge. Unsurprisingly, it's almost entirely packed for the next two weeks between work and volunteer events.

"Are you free in two weeks?" I ask hesitantly. "Sorry, there's just a ton of stuff going on this week, and Saturday is the community scavenger hunt that Jo, Vic, and the Queer Quips host every year."

Ashe stands and walks around the couch back to the barstool where he left his jacket. "It's no problem, L. Two weeks it is."

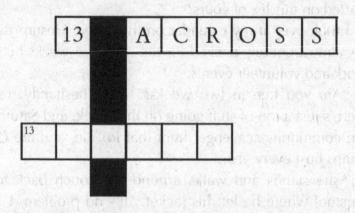

13 ACROSS

You can't have this without a woven
basket and a gingham tablecloth.

October 11, 2024

Once a season, Jo, Vic, Mira, and I get together for a "picnic
with the peeps." Even better, we challenge ourselves to come
up and stick with a theme for our attire and the food we
bring. Today's theme: *Friends of Dorothy*. We have an anon-
ymous poll going, so none of us know what character anyone
else is going to be. We just know which characters are left to
choose from.

And that's how I find myself strolling through Centennial
Park with a faux fur jacket, glued-on whiskers, and amateurly
applied graphic eyeliner on. I swing my blue-and-white ging-
ham-lined picnic basket that I packed with different kinds of
cheeses and meats as I strut toward my friends at the table.

Mira is dressed head to toe in silver, complete with a shiny
top hat headband. She clearly chose the tin man. Jo, on the

E. A. M. Trofimenkoff

other hand, has a pair of oversized denim overalls on top of a blue plaid button-up. Their short blonde hair is even spiked up to give an extra illusion of being the scarecrow. The only other character left was the wizard, but as I turn to take in Vic's costume, I'm not quite convinced that's what they went for . . . They're a bit too . . . green? Their face and arms are painted, and even though their black cloak covers most of them, I can still see the hint of green on their neck and chest as well.

"Shigo?" I ask, knowing full well this will get a reaction out of them.

As predicted, Vic scoffs and rolls their eyes. "Wrong universe, L."

I shrug. "A thembo can dream," I say as I take my spot next to them and place my basket on the table.

"Vic went a bit overboard with the green," Jo says as they open the box of snacks they brought.

"You know what—I like Elphaba better anyway," Vic says as they cross their arms over their chest. The black witch hat shifts on their head, but they make no effort to correct it.

Mira giggles. "But I thought we were supposed to be *friends* of Dorothy."

"There's just no pleasing, y'all," Vic huffs. But there's a tilt of amusement on their lips that gives away the ruse.

We spread out a checkered tablecloth and lay out the food we brought. My mouth waters when I see that Mira has brought some of her Kokum's famous bannock and jerky. Vic and Jo place an assorted platter of berries surrounding a towering Kransekake that's been decorated in icing. Each ring has four raspberries on it, making it look like a white Christmas tree with red balls.

"And Jo went overboard with the cake," Vic says with a hint of victory in their voice. "I mean, this isn't a wedding. We already had one of those."

"I'd marry you," I say as I sneak a piece of the delicious cake.

"Me too," Mira agrees, following my movements.

"Thank you." Jo smirks and pops a raspberry in their mouth. "Now if only L could win the Elusive Echo so we could have some cash for a ceremony."

I give them a half-hearted smirk. "Hey, don't mock the very ambiguous and not at all straightforward puzzle that occupies my every morning," I tease.

The four of us take turns making our plates, and, like always, we begin comparing notes on our most recent reads.

"What about you, L?" Mira asks.

I sigh. "Not much to report," I say as I chase a grape around with my fork.

"Oh no! Reading slump?"

I look up to find Jo leaning forward slightly, resting their elbows on the table. "A deep one," I say, defeated.

"Don't fret over it too much," Vic offers, giving me a gentle nudge with their shoulder. "We've all been there. Plus, there's not much real estate available in your brain right now. It's okay to prioritize something else."

"Thanks," I say as I bump them back.

"Speaking of, how's the list coming along? Anything we can help with?"

I reach into the pocket of my coat and pull out the folded paper. "It's pretty short," I admit as I flatten it in front of me.

My friends lean over to inspect, taking their time to read each item on the list.

"Laser tag?" Mira asks, eyebrows furrowed.

I let out a nervous laugh. "That one is Ashe's request," I say.

All three of them sit back and exchange a glance with each other.

"That's so cute!" Mira's voice seems to have raised an entire octave in the span of a single breath.

"Yeah," I say sarcastically. "Nothing says cute like getting bombarded by children in a dark room filled with obstacles."

"It could be worse. They could be chickens," Jo adds.

An image of a flock of chickens armed with laser guns flashes through my mind and I can't help but giggle.

"I still think I'd rather take the chickens."

We all laugh.

"You don't have a nature walk on your list," Vic points out.

I look back down at the paper. They're right.

"What would I do without you?" I ask as I search for a pen in my purse.

Vic shrugs. "You know I'll always have your back," they say. "We could take advantage of the park if you don't mind us joining you? And we can make sure everything looks okay for the Queer Quips' scavenger hunt tomorrow while we're there."

I give the three of them a soft smile. "I'd be delighted."

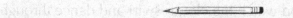

I can't imagine how strange the four of us look basking in the afternoon sun dressed as Dorothy's entourage. Mira is at the top of the waterfall inspecting the late-season flowers. Her silver top hat headband has fallen to the front of her head, but she's too focused on the world in front of her to push it back. Jo and Vic sit across the water from me, sharing the same rock, placing petals in each other's hair. One side of Jo's coveralls has come undone, leaving the front hanging in over their chest at a lopsided angle. When Vic reaches over to fix it, there's a warmth that seems to glow between the two of them. I can't help but let it play over my skin and flow through my veins as well.

One thing they never told us growing up is how important the friends you have in your twenties would be. The four of us have grown together, broken together, cried together, and laughed together, and somehow always stayed together. They're more my family than most of my blood relatives.

But what if they leave? What if it's been a lie all along? the gremlins whisper.

I take a deep breath, and for the first time, try something new. I've always fought them, rebutted, and pushed back. But maybe that's not what they need. Maybe that's not what *I* need.

"No," I tell them, gently. "It's not. They love us and I love them. And even if it is a lie, it was still worth it to give a part of my heart to them. They taught me that it's okay to be un-apologetically myself, and accepted and embraced me when I did. That's not something a fake friend would do. So no," I say again, trying to wrap my mind in a strong embrace, "our friendship isn't a lie. Not even close. It's a gift."

The four of us sit together in relative silence. I lie back on the soft grass and watch the clouds swirl and dance through the sky. Only the soft sounds of the water washing over the rocks accompanies us. My fingers play through the cool earth beneath me, and I imagine the threads of life reaching up and wrapping us all in a tender embrace. Is this joy? I'm not sure. But it's a close second: peace.

"... L? L?"

I open my eyes to find my friends standing over me. When did I close them?

"You okay?" Mira asks.

I suck in a breath that fills my belly and my lungs. "Never better."

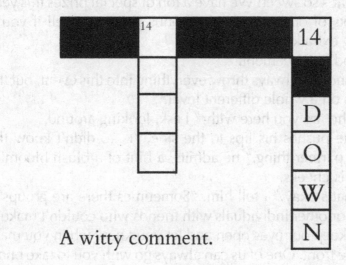

A witty comment.

October 12, 2024

A choir of excited voices echoes around us as we welcome everyone to this year's fundraiser. Jo and Vic are both dressed in their Queer Quips T-shirts that feature magnifying glasses for the Q's, a rainbow circling the words. Jo scans each pair in as Vic distributes the community passports with the scavenger hunt information on it to the people in the lineup. Mira and I are also in matching shirts. The two of us walk down the line, making sure everyone is paired and paid, with everything ready to show Jo once they reach the front of the line.

My eyes catch on a familiar figure toward the end.

"Ashe?" I ask as we approach him. "What are you doing here?"

He runs his tongue over his teeth behind his lips. "I figured this would be a good way to learn more about the town. And support a good cause, of course," he says as he gestures at my shirt.

"That's so sweet! We have a ton of special prizes this year, and lots of opportunities for bonus points as well if you're feeling extra keen," Mira says.

I nod in agreement.

Jo and Vic always throw everything into this event, but this year is on a whole different level.

"Who are you here with?" I ask, looking around.

Ashe pushes his lips to the side. "I . . . didn't know this was a partner thing," he admits, a hint of a blush blooming over his cheeks.

"That's okay," I tell him. "Sometimes there are groups of three, or other individuals with friends who couldn't make it. We'll keep our eyes open and let you know when you make it to the front. One of us can always go with you to take photo evidence if you need. We'll figure it out."

Ashe nods and grins at us. "Thanks."

When he finally reaches Jo, Ashe looks around at the lack of people.

"No stragglers?" he asks.

"Not this year," Vic says, handing him a passport. "But that's okay. L can go with you. They know the town like the back of their hand."

It's true. And I'd be lying if I said I wasn't excited to show him around my hometown.

"Are you sure?" I ask.

They wave their hands in front of them dismissively. "We have it under control. Go. Have some *fun*."

The teasing tone in their voice doesn't go unnoticed. As soon as I told them about my "fun" comment, I knew I wouldn't live it down.

I roll my eyes and wave goodbye at them before leading Ashe down the road to Charlie. Once we're buckled in, Ashe opens up the folded page.

The paper is decorated with the classic yellow airplane on the bottom right corner, a huge cinnamon bun and a coffee on the bottom left, and the top corners are covered with flowers, books, and a movie reel lacing through the petals and the pages. Below the Queer Quips title, there are twenty stops, highlighting some amazing places around town.

- Take a photo of yourself with the yellow airplane at the end of 4th street
- Head on down to Flowers on Fifth and ask for a daisy
- Bring the daisy to Paul's Place, and trade it in for a "Bite of Bun"
- Make your way to The Fox Den and answer the puzzle for bonus points
- Check out the new releases down at the Video Place and play "Guess the Budget"

The list continues all the way down the page with empty boxes to the left of each item to be stamped or stickered. At the end it tells us to download the Quips app for a digital scrapbook documenting the scavenger hunt and to have a nice adventure. There's a final section at the bottom of the page highlighting that each year, the Quips raise about two thousand dollars through the scavenger hunt and they donate every penny to the breakfast program at the elementary school, making it one of the most successful short-term fundraisers the town has ever seen.

"Two thousand dollars?" Ashe remarks. "That's a lot of money."

I put the car in reverse and back up out of my parking spot.

"Jo and Vic never do anything half-assed," I say. "Full ass only."

I laugh and realize too late that Ashe isn't laughing with me.

Embarrassment floods my cheeks.

"Sorry, that's not supposed to be as crude as it sounds," I say as I turn down the alleyway to the next street.

At the stop sign, I turn and see Ashe barely holding back what I can only assume is a hysterical bout of giggles.

"What?" I ask, relieved to see amusement and not a what-the-fuck expression on his face.

Not a second later, he lets out the gentlest whistle of a laugh, as if there isn't enough air in his lungs to properly support him.

"Are you okay?"

Ashe waves a hand in front of his face and sucks in a breath. "Sorry," he finally says, wiping a small tear from his eye. "I just don't think I've ever heard someone refer to their friends as 'full asses' and mean it in such a loving way."

I nudge him with my elbow as we near the next intersection.

"Careful," I say teasingly. "I might just call you an ass too."

Ashe lets out another final laugh.

"That's okay," he says. "I'd be honored."

"There really is a giant yellow airplane," Ashe says as he looks up at it.

"There used to be a NATO training program here," I tell him. "A lot of them flew planes like this."

Ashe walks over to read the bronze memorial on the base holding the plane. The wind blows through his black long-sleeve shirt, making small ripples along his back. His fingers play at the loose bottom of the fabric, holding it close to his belt.

"Do you know much about airplanes?" he asks.

I shake my head and then realize he can't see me with his back turned.

"No," I admit. "You?"

"Not a thing," he says. "I was more of a bicycle kid. You know, the closer to the ground, the less distance to fall." He rubs at his elbow as if nursing it. "Didn't keep me from getting my share of bumps and bruises though."

"At least you learned from them?"

Ashe turns and gives me a wry smile. "I wish I could agree." Then he raises his arms out to the side and kicks a leg out, imitating the plane above him. "Photo?"

I bring out my phone, open the Quips app and click on Ashe's profile before taking the picture of him smiling like a kid in a candy store, arms outstretched as if he too were flying in the wind.

"Okay," I say, bringing out the paper, "where to next?"

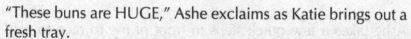

"These buns are HUGE," Ashe exclaims as Katie brings out a fresh tray.

He twirls the head of the daisy between his fingers as he gawks at the fresh cinnamon buns. Flowers on Fifth was extremely busy, but Ashe's presence sparked a sizzling conversation between the patrons. I overheard a few people talking about "a scandalous new city boy" and "where is he from," among many others. A symptom of being the new kid in town, I guess.

"Only a bite," I remind him, pointing at the scavenger hunt page.

Ashe lets out a low breath. "I'm not sure I could have any more than that anyway."

He trades the white flower for a piece of the dessert dripping in cream cheese icing. My mouth waters at the smell.

"Here," he says, passing me a fork. "There's plenty for the both of us."

I take it gratefully and split the cinnamon bun in half before taking out my phone again. I change it to the front-facing camera and get the perfect picture of the two of us, mouths wide open, anticipating the treat on our forks.

Ashe's cheeks are full as he chews, giving him the appearance of a satisfied chipmunk, and it takes all the self-control I have not to spit out the dessert from laughter. It's too tasty to sacrifice, but I have to be extra careful not to pass it through my nose either.

I hold a hand in front of my mouth as I finish my piece and let out a giggle.

"How'd you eat so fast?" Ashe mumbles through his full mouth.

"Years and years of practice," I tell him.

Ashe takes a few quick steps in front of me to race toward The Fox Den.

"I've driven past this so many times and always wondered what was inside. I always thought it was a bar or something."

The outside of the building is the shape of a giant tree stump. The double doors for the entrance, like the siding, are wood and arched as if to create the illusion of entering a fairy house. Ashe pulls the doors open to reveal the familiar small, cozy restaurant. Strands of amber twinkle lights decorate the roof like stars, and ivy vines cover the walls from floor to ceiling. The glass refrigerator on the north side of the building is home to a dozen different kinds of ice cream, which is a popular treat year-round. There's a wooden counter with an old cash register on it, and a welcome sign for the Queer Quips participants.

"Hey y'all!" Trix says in her thick southern drawl. "Part o' the hunt?"

"Yes, ma'am," I reply, handing her our page.

The petite woman takes out a fox sticker from under the counter and places it over the empty box next to The Fox Den item on our passport.

"There y'all go." She wipes her hands off on her apron. "You kids wanna try your hands at a game for some extra points?" Her springy blonde curls bounce as she pushes a word search puzzle our way. "If you can find the three words of our name in here, then I'll give y'all an extra sticker."

I look over to Ashe. "You want to give it a go?" I ask him.

He leans over, and the soft smell of freshly baked cinnamon buns hits my nose again, making my stomach grumble.

"Uh oh, can't leave here on an empty stomach," Trixie says. "The usual?"

Before I have a chance to reply, she spins on her heels and makes her way toward the kitchen behind her.

"Darl, one order of sour cream and chive fries," she orders.

"Coming right up!" a low voice replies.

"There," Ashe says, circling "FOX" with his fingers.

"Can we write on this, Trix?"

She comes back and tosses a pen on the counter. "Of course, hun. There's plenty where that came from."

By the time my fries are ready, we've found "THE FOX DEN" in the puzzle. I turn the paper back around to Trix and she rewards us with another sticker.

"Thanks," I say as I bring out my wallet.

"Never mind your cash, dear," she says. "This one's on the house. Consider it a thank-you for all you do in your classroom."

I blush and nod my head to her. "Thanks, Trix, but I'll get you next time," I say as I wag a finger at her.

She waves back, shooing us out of the shop. "You can try!"

Some of the stops were easy: hopscotch on the sidewalk outside the high school, fencing with sticks at the top of one of the skate park ramps, and finding ten pieces of garbage around town. Others required much more thought and effort. Like hanging upside down on the monkey bars at the Lion's Park.

"We don't have to," I say looking down at the paper. "It's optional."

Ashe fiddles with the end of his shirt. "I think I'll skip this one," he says. Something flashes behind his eyes, and I notice that his shoulders have come up closer to his ears. Maybe he's cold.

"I have an extra jacket in the car," I offer.

He shakes his head. "I'm okay," he says. "What's the other option?"

I nod toward the train part of the play structure with the "Lion's Club" logo on the front. "Take a picture upside down on the monkey bars or with the train."

"Do we get points if we do both?" he asks.

I shrug. "No idea. But it's worth a shot?"

I grip the cold metal with both hands and let myself hang. What the hell do I think I'm doing? At the very least I am going to wake up with some very sore muscles. When was the last time I even attempted something like this? Twenty years ago? Yikes.

I tighten my grip as I try to bring my legs up, but it's no use.

"Can you . . . give me a . . . hand?" I ask Ashe.

He wraps an arm under my knees for support. It's enough to lace one foot through. If I could just get my other one . . .

"Ha!" I say as I put my other foot through the bars. I hesitantly let go, allowing my upper body to fall toward the ground.

Which was a complete miscalculation. Twenty years ago, I was a child. And now I am . . . not. Which means my breasts, which were previously nonexistent, are now threatening to strangle the life out of me as I dangle upside down from a metal bar at a children's playground. Great. Fantastic. Can't wait for this to be featured in my obituary.

"Take the picture," I rasp.

My glasses fall to my forehead and I try to manage a smile and two peace signs as I hold my breath and hope I can get down in time.

"Got it," he says. "Need some help down?"

"What does . . . it look . . . like?" I say, reaching back up for the bars.

Ashe lets out a low laugh as he places an arm on my back to help me. I suck in a deep breath once my boobs fall back to their normal place on my body.

I look over to find Ashe biting his lips together to keep him from laughing.

I try to scowl back. "It's not funny!" But I can't help the smile that dares to creep across my face. "Just help me get down from here, will you?"

The last stop is at the Continuing Care Center. We walk in through the front doors to find a large audience of patients welcoming us. Their wheelchairs are lined up in rows extending all the way back past the old piano on the north wall into the main hallway. The gold evening light dances through the windows that line the perimeter of the foyer, giving the residents an ethereal glow.

"Welcome!" a short Black man says as he walks around the reception table. "Are we your last stop on the Quips scavenger hunt?"

The man is dressed in a fun flamingo shirt. Each of the pink birds is wearing a pair of sunglasses, and their legs and wings are stretched out in different poses, making them look as if they're dancing. The name tag on his shirt reads, "George".

Ashe and I nod.

"Hear that, folks? Let's make this something special for the young couple, okay?"

Before I have a chance to open my mouth and correct him, the man turns around and thrusts a microphone into each of our hands.

I look down at the tiny web of silver crisscrosses staring back at me. "What's this for?" I ask, unsure of whether I want to know the answer or not.

"A lot of our friends here have hearing problems, so this is just to help."

The knot in my stomach loosens. Thank the Universe it wasn't for—

My thoughts disappear like smoke on the wind as the man brings forward a wheeling cart complete with a projector and some kind of other mechanical box.

"Please don't tell me we're singing karaoke to a bunch of seniors," Ashe leans over and whispers in my ear.

I clench my teeth together, unable to answer.

"Okay!" George says enthusiastically. "What song would we like to sing?"

"Sorry," I say, finally finding my voice again. "Is there—"

"Johnny Cash!" a low voice booms from the back of the room, interrupting me.

"Elvis!" The woman's squeaky tone pierces through my brain so hard, I swear I can feel it in the back of my eyes.

"Doreen, we had Elvis with the last group," George says, softly.

"Yes, well, I want another song!"

"Elton John!" someone else calls out.

George turns around to face us.

"What will it be?" he asks.

Ashe and I exchange a glance.

A few months ago, Iris gave me an assignment to find things that scare me and don't put me in any form of physical danger. I horribly failed, at least in my eyes. She just said I might not have been ready for it, and we put it on the back shelf.

Standing here, though, is terrifying. I don't sing, unless you count my opera-worthy shower performances, which, for the record, should absolutely *not* be counted. I take a look around the room. Physical danger? Definitely not. I guess someone could throw a cane at us if we're particularly bad, but other than that, the worst that could happen is we get booed with all the passion of a snob mob. But they don't look like the type. In fact, everyone seems delighted, excited even, to have another performance on their doorstep.

"Well?" George asks again.

I finally spare a glance at Ashe, who appears to be just as paralyzed as I feel.

"I don't think I can do this," he says. His fingers work the bottom of his shirt, twisting it in knots. His face has lost nearly all its color, and his eyes look like they might bulge out of his head at any second.

"You don't have to," I reassure him. This is just a game, after all.

Ashe's eyes turn down to the pink-and-white tiled floor.

"Okay," he says, and takes a slight step back.

I close my eyes and try to feel the hard floor beneath my feet.

It's just a song, I remind myself.

"Hi folks," I say, surprised at the clarity of my voice. I don't dare stop now. "I'm L. I'll be singing for you today, but I'm not much of a singer, so I'm going to need some help. Do you think you can do that?"

The crowd immediately echoes sounds of joy as they cheer in unison. I raise my hand up to quiet them down.

"Thank you," I say, and turn to George. "Let's do 'Don't Go Breaking My Heart.'"

A wide grin extends across his face. "A classic."

He types something into his computer, and a few moments later, the YouTube screen pops up on the projector behind the residents.

"They won't be able to see the lyrics there," I tell George.

He waves my concerns away.

"They know them, *trust me.*" He says the last part in a way that insinuates much more than those two words could possibly hold.

As the intro music begins to play, I feel my palms start to sweat. My heart rate is through the roof. And if you asked my brain whether I was about to deliver a subpar vocal performance or was currently being chased by wolves, I'm not sure they would give you the real answer.

The beginning words show up on the screen. I suck in a breath and sing.

The residents and I immediately fall into the familiar back-and-forth of the song. A few bars in, I sense movement to my side. To my surprise, Ashe has walked back up. His hand grips the microphone in an unbreakable vice. His knuckles threaten to push through his skin from the force, and his arm shakes from the effort. His voice is quiet. It's definitely not loud enough for everyone else to hear, but I can. And although he's no professional, his tone is low and calm. I'm not sure why or how, but it steadies me too.

The song ends and our audience claps. A few people in the back rise from their chairs to give us a standing ovation. Ashe and I bow awkwardly and thank everyone for their patience with us.

"You can turn your hearing aids back on," George says, gesturing to his ears.

At least half of the residents follow his gesture.

"What?" I say, gawking at him.

He shrugs. "Most of them can't hear a thing even with the aids. You kids did great, though. Here." He stamps our passport in the final spot. "I hope you two have a good night. Be safe out there!"

When Ashe and I make it back to the car, I can still feel the adrenaline coursing through my veins. It's a high like I haven't felt in ages.

Ashe holds his hands out in front of his body. They're shaking like the fall leaves threatening to let loose in the breeze.

"You okay?" I ask him.

A nervous laugh escapes his lips. "Well, we didn't have karaoke or scavenger hunt on the childhood bucket list originally, but we clearly should have because that was a blast," he says, grinning.

I stare at the man, wide-eyed and curious. What happened to the Ashe from ten minutes ago? The one who didn't want to speak into the microphone, let alone sing.

"What—"

"The song," he says. He turns his body to face me. A crooked grin plays at his lips. "Nan used to sing it to me when I was a kid and couldn't sleep. Today"—he looks down at his shaking fingers—"it was like . . . having a piece of her again." When he brings his eyes back up to meet my gaze, they're shiny with the promise of tears. "Thank you."

The breath catches in my throat. I can't speak, so I nod instead. Then I pull out the childhood bucket list from my pocket and write *QQ SH* in my loose handwriting before crossing it out immediately after.

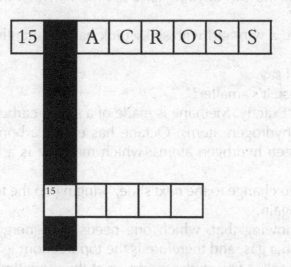

| 15 | ■ | A | C | R | O | S | S |

| 15 | | | | |

An attempt to understand
a new concept.

October 14, 2024

One of the things about living in Alberta is that it always comes back to oil. Even the person on the Elusive Echo this morning guessed that it was the clang of an oil rig. They were unfortunately incorrect. I'm not surprised when I bring up the general layers and products that come from fracking that nearly half the class already knows what the process is and why it's done. The rest of them catch on easily, and we can move on to why each of the different fractions come out when they do.

"Who can tell me which molecule is lighter, methane or octane?"

Predictably, Maggie raises her hand in the air, excitedly, and I nod my head to her, giving her permission to answer.

"Methane."

"Great! And can anybody else tell me why that might be the case?"

Jordana, a wiry girl with spiky pink hair, hesitantly raises her arm.

"Yes?" I say.

"Because it's smaller?"

I nod. "Exactly. Methane is made of a single carbon atom and four hydrogen atoms. Octane has eight carbon atoms and eighteen hydrogen atoms, which means it is a lot bigger."

I click to change to the next slide, bringing up the fracking diagram again.

"So, knowing that, which one needs less energy to be turned into a gas, and therefore is the top fraction?"

"Methane!" a few students answer at the same time.

"Great!" I look at the clock. We still have about five minutes left. More than enough time for me to cover alternatives.

I change the slide again. "Now, there are other interesting ways of obtaining oil, such as through algae. Does anyone know what algae is?"

"Isn't that the green stuff in the lakes?" Maggie asks.

"Yes, it is," I say. "But did you know that algae is good for a ton of things? I mean, it's not good to swim in, obviously, but it's so important for the earth. It captures carbon dioxide from the atmosphere, and it can even provide nutrients to different kinds of fish and other organisms that live in the water with it. But," I continue, flipping to the last slide, "it can also be used to make oil!" I say excitedly.

I've lost some students, which isn't surprising, but there are still a few paying close attention to what I'm saying, so I continue.

"Unfortunately, the process still needs very high pressures and temperatures to work, but it's a promising alternative to the fracking process, and might even provide some interesting job opportunities for you in the future! If you're interested, I have a pamphlet with some extra information on it. Just something to think about after graduation. A lot of these companies have hands-on training, and some of them are even willing to help pay for your tuition if you need any post-secondary credentials."

The bell rings, and my students pack away their notebooks. I leave a stack of the pamphlets at the desk near the door. Most of them walk by, but I'm pleased to see a few pick them up.

I carefully gather my things and make my way toward Silva's office. My steps feel lighter as I walk down the familiar halls. I always feel better after teaching. I guess I'm one of the privileged few who found their calling early and ran with it. I can't imagine what life would be like if I didn't have my classroom or my students. Just the thought of it threatens to cloud my mind with darkness.

I knock on Silva's door a few times before entering.

"Ah, L," the silver-haired woman says as she greets me. "Come, sit." She gestures at the many different chairs in the room.

I decide on the recliner in the corner.

The school counselor closes the door and sits behind her desk again. "I have a few things for you to think about," she says, assembling a stack of papers into a file. She hands it to me, and I take it gratefully.

"Of course I can't share any personal information about Tobe with you, but I can say that he tends to struggle with verbal communication if he's stressed. Have you considered using a form of sign language?"

"Sign language?" I ask, confused.

She nods her head. "Yes, he's used it a few times in our sessions. It seems . . . easier for him."

It had never occurred to me that using a different language might be better for Tobe. But then again, isn't that what we were already trying without actually having a label on it?

"I've included a few different resources in that file, including some information on classes being taught at the Lethbridge College campus here in town. It's twice a week. Unfortunately the class has already started, but I know the instructor. I might be able to get you in if you're interested and willing to put in a little extra work to catch up."

For the benefit of my students? I'd do anything.

"Thank you, Silva."

"It's my pleasure, dear." She looks over at her monitor and straightens slightly. "Oh, I almost forgot."

She clicks a button and the printer starts working on something at the side of her desk. "You were asking about alternative evaluation methods the other day, and I came across some interesting research papers. I have a list of them here." She picks up the paper and hands it to me.

There are about ten different titles on the page. Plenty of reading material to keep me occupied during my preparation period.

"Thank you again," I say as I place the paper in the file.

"Like I said, it's my pleasure. You're dedicated to your students, L. I see that, and I'd like to help where I can. Hopefully this is a good start."

I place the file in my bag, and stand. "I'll let you know how it goes." I make my way back to the door, twisting the knob. "Have a good day, Silva."

"You too, dear. Take care! Buh-bye now!"

I close the door behind me and take a look down the hall to make sure I'm not going to run into anyone. My eyes immediately land on Ashe, who is leaning over helping a student pick up their papers which are scattered all over the floor.

He lifts his gaze to mine. When he recognizes me, I get a warm smile and a wave.

"Hey, L," he says as I approach.

"Everything okay over here?" I ask.

Ashe and the student nod.

"Just lost my grip," they say. "I had to take extra assignments for a friend who's sick."

"That's very nice of you," I tell them. "Here, maybe this will help."

I take out the papers from Silva and place them in my bag, offering the empty file folder to the student.

"Oh, thank you!" they say appreciatively as they tuck the assignments away. "I better get to class. I'm sooooo late. Uh, thanks again!"

Before Ashe or I have a chance to say anything back, the student flies down the hall to the last room on the right.

I laugh. "Kind of reminds me of me when I was that age," I say.

"Oh?" Ashe raises a brow at me.

"Yeah, awkward, a bit disorganized, trying to do too many things at once. Oh wait." I laugh again. "That sounds like me now, too."

Ashe's welcoming grin returns to his face. "There are certainly worse people to be compared to."

I smirk. "Careful, Ashe, that almost sounded like a compliment."

"That's because it was meant to be one."

I can't help the blush that spreads through my cheeks. I look down at my feet, hoping it goes away without him noticing.

"What's that you have there?" he asks.

My stomach twists. He's calling me out on my embarrassing reaction.

But when I look back up, I see him pointing at the papers in my bag.

I let out a low breath. "Oh, just some homework," I tell him.

"Homework? I thought you were the teacher."

"Yeah, well, lifelong student and all that. Doesn't hurt to exercise old muscles. Or new ones, I guess."

"New ones?" he asks.

"Yeah, Silva thinks it might be good to learn sign language for one of my students."

Ashe's eyes brighten. "ASL?"

I nod. "I guess so. There's some classes at the college she thinks I should register for, but it's already a few weeks into the semester, so I'm going to be a bit behind, if I get in at all."

Ashe pinches his lips to the side. "What if I told you I knew ASL?"

"You do?" I ask.

He runs a hand through his untied hair. "Yeah, my best friend back in high school was deaf. His whole family was, actually."

"Was?" I ask, hesitantly.

"Is," he clarifies. "We just haven't talked much in the last few years. You know, life gets busy and well . . . sometimes you lose touch."

"May I give you a reassuring squeeze?" I ask.

He smiles and nods, letting me take his arm.

"Maybe you should reach out again some time."

Ashe looks off to the end of the hall. "Yeah, maybe."

I get the sense that he probably doesn't want to talk about this anymore, so instead I ask him, "Any chance you'd like to play teacher instead of me?"

I get a wry smile in response. "Role-play? So early on into our friendship?" he teases, bringing his hand up to rest over his heart, letting his jaw drop dramatically.

"Oh, shut up." I let go of his arm. "I'd like to walk into this ASL class with at least a little bit of knowledge under my belt, if I can."

Oh for the love of everything good in the world, please don't make a comment about being under my belt.

Ashe looks at me for a few moments as if he's debating it.

Don't say it, I challenge him through my stare.

"Sure," he finally says. "But on one condition."

"And that is?" I ask.

"I'll trade you. For a lesson in chemistry."

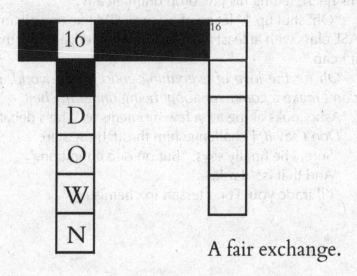

A fair exchange.

October 14, 2024

"I feel like I'm in detention," Ashe says. He pulls at the bottom of his loose black T-shirt as he takes his seat.

He's in the front desk where Maggie usually sits with a few pieces of scrap paper in front of him.

There's a bad boy comment in there somewhere.

Shut up.

"It's better to have the whiteboard space," I say instead.

Ashe clicks his pen and stares up at me.

"So . . . what do you want to know?" I ask.

"Hmm . . . where does human consciousness come from?"

I shake my head and put my hands on my hips. "About chemistry, Ashe," I scold.

He shrugs. "You asked."

I don't relent. I continue giving him an unimpressed stare.

"Okay, fine. How about . . . cars?"

"Cars?" I ask.

"Yeah, it's how we met, kind of. So tell me something about cars. Gas?"

"Okay," I say, moving to the whiteboard. "Well, before we get into that, we should talk about what makes up gasoline. And yes, I mean that there are many different compounds in it. One of them that you've probably heard of is octane?"

I turn around to see Ashe nodding his head.

"Good, so octane—let's just focus on octane—is your fuel source, right? And obviously it burns. But it needs oxygen to burn."

I write down "octane" and "oxygen" on the board and draw an arrow after them.

"When the octane burns, well, when any hydrocarbon burns, it produces carbon dioxide—yes, the same gas we breathe out, and water."

I write the products down on the right-hand side of the arrow and turn back around.

"This is called a combustion reaction, and you always get the same products, no matter what kind of hydrocarbon fuel you start with."

"Hydrocarbon?" Ashe asks.

"It's a compound made of hydrogen, hence the hydro, and carbon. We won't worry about the specifics of that unless you want to. I was thinking of staying more big-picture here if that's okay."

He nods. "Sure, sounds good."

"Great, well, like I said, carbon dioxide and water are the products in this reaction. Both of them are gasses at this temperature. Now, I'm not a mechanic or an engineer, so I can't give you any specifics, but gasses are larger in volume than liquids, so when the octane is ignited, it expands, causing the piston in the engine to move. And that's all I got. If you want more, you'll have to talk with Heather in shop class."

Ashe laughs. "I'm sure I'd be knee-deep in grease by the end of the session."

"Fair, but I bet you'd come out learning more than you expected."

"And I'm sure I'd have a few scars to prove it too." He looks back up at the board. "I've heard a lot of talk about hydrogen power instead of gas. Does that work the same?"

I move my head from side to side. "Kind of? It's still combustion, if that's what you're asking. But instead of getting carbon dioxide as a byproduct, all you get is water."

Ashe squints at the board, and I swear I can almost see the wheels turning in his brain.

"And that's because instead of having a"—he pinches his lips together in a line as if mentally searching for something—"hybercarbon, you just have hydrogen?"

So close!

"Hydrocarbon," I gently correct. "And yes, that's exactly why. No carbon? No carbon dioxide. Can't make something out of nothing. That's the law of conservation of mass."

Ashe writes down a few notes and then clicks his pen.

I sit down at the desk next to him. "Is there anything I should read or watch or anything before we do some ASL?"

Ashe shakes his head. "I think it's better if we just get into it. And since most of us start off by learning how to read by learning the alphabet, maybe we should start there for sign language too? I mean, that's how Zander taught me."

"Zander?" I ask.

"My, uh, friend."

Oh, shit, of course.

"Oh right," I say and give him an embarrassed laugh. "So, what's 'A'?"

Ashe raises a fist to his side. Except it's not quite a fist. His fingers are folded down but not curled around. I do my best to copy the movement.

"Good, now 'B.'"

He opens his hand to me and places his thumb across his palm. I look back and forth between my hand and his to make sure they look the same. Or as close to the same as they can be.

We continue through until we reach "M."

"This one can be a bit of a stretch," he says, holding out a fist similar to what he showed me for "A" except his thumb is gone now. Under his fingers?

I look at my fist and try to twist my fingers the same way he has his, but I have no idea where my thumb is supposed to go, and before I know it, I'm all twisted up.

"Here, let me help," Ashe says as he takes my hand.

Everything goes still and flat. I am suddenly very aware of my heart beating in my chest, and oh shit, are my palms sweaty? Am I clammy? Do I smell? Am I too rigid? Fuck, am I making this weird?

Ashe's lips are moving and he's placing his hand over mine and trying to twist my thumb. I tense.

"Is everything okay?" he asks.

We are very close together. His eyes have just a hint of green in them, and the light from the room seems to make the amber flecks shine. And he's warm. And soft. His hands aren't calloused in the slightest. I can feel every hair on my arm stand on end. And I realize that if I can see these things about him, he can probably see the giant breaths I am taking and can definitely feel how I am a jittering mess too.

"Sorry," I say, pulling my hand away and leaning back. "I'm just . . . uh . . . really thirsty." I reach over and take a long drink of water. When I'm done, I feel somewhat like myself again.

"You were saying?" I manage through a raspy voice.

Ashe runs a hand through his messy hair and clears his throat. "Yes, uh, 'M.' Can you try it again?"

I raise my shaking hand and do my best to stretch my thumb over. This time with much more success than my first attempt.

"Good, now 'N' is basically the same, but one finger over."

I follow again and again and again, copying his motions, but somehow my mind wanders back to that moment. I'm not a "touchy" person, so his contact probably just sent my nervous system into overdrive. I ignore the other physiological effects. Probably just a sign of stress, right? I'm overworked and taking on more than I should. This just sent me overboard.

Reassured that I have not completely lost my mind, I find myself making a 'Z' with my pointer finger through the air when we reach the end of the alphabet.

"And that's it," Ashe says. "Congrats, you can spell in ASL now."

And I can also completely lose my cool at the slightest touch, yay!

"If I can remember the letters," I reply.

"You'll get there," he reassures me. "I'm sure you didn't learn how to read in a day. It's just practice. Like anything else."

"Just practice," I repeat.

We work through the alphabet a second time. By the end, it feels like I've done an intense version of finger yoga. Is that a thing?

I clench and unclench my fists, trying to stretch my fingers out. "So . . . Zander?"

Ashe gives me a hesitant look. "Yeah," he sighs. "It's a long story involving a teenage crush on my part and a kiss that sent our friendship into a . . . weird place."

"Ah," I say nodding. Been there. Done that.

"It was . . . awkward after that," he admits. "Being a teenager is weird."

"You can say that again."

Ashe rubs his thumb along the inside of his other hand. "I still think of him though. Not in that way, of course," he adds quickly. "It's just . . . I miss how easy it was being friends with him. But then again, maybe I just miss how easy it was being a kid."

I push my glasses up my nose and study him. "Maybe he thinks the same," I tell him.

Ashe shrugs. "Maybe. Maybe not. Either way, it's been years. I wouldn't know where to pick things up again."

He glances at the clock. "Have time for one more round?" he asks.

I square my shoulders and nod. "Let's do this."

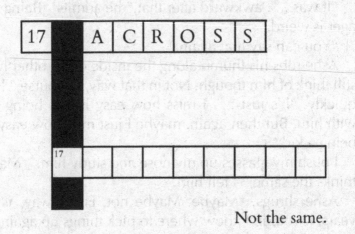

Not the same.

October 19, 2024

No amount of Advil and heat packs could possibly stop this war that is raging in my uterus right now.

   I had planned on continuing with my chaotic thought board, but annoyingly, this bleeding body had other ideas. As it turned out, the list of resources that Silva provided me with was like a gold mine of alternative assessment strategies and techniques. Fortunately I enjoy deep-diving into material like this. Unfortunately, the further I went, the deeper I got, with no end in sight. Just when I thought I might have had a complete comprehensive list, I found something else. And that something else led to another option, and then another. By the end, I had a messy map that looked like it could have been constructed by a crazed teen in a horror film trying to put the pieces together. And that's when it hit me. Perhaps mapping concepts like this wasn't a bad idea at all. A trip to the dollar store and a few coffees later, I finally had a plan for how to include all of my students in an accessible evaluation strategy. Or at least what I hoped would be.

My phone buzzes with a text prompt and I groan as I roll over on the couch to look at it. When the screen lights up with a message from Ashe, my heart sinks.

Fuck. We were supposed to go do laser tag today.

I can barely get off this couch, let alone go get chased around by a bunch of kids.

But what if he thinks I'm ditching our first official item on the childhood bucket list?

I close my eyes and take a deep breath.

And I'm rewarded with another sharp stab of pain.

I grind my teeth together and dig my nails into my palms as I ride through the wave.

No. I really can't do this.

I swallow my pride and my fears, type out the most heartfelt apology message I can muster, press send, and fall back onto the couch.

Nox jumps up a moment later, and it doesn't take long for Nyx to follow. Nox makes soft kneads on my sore belly as her sister settles between my legs. Slowly, their symphony of purrs fills the air. Whoever says that cats aren't responsive to their humans has clearly never owned a cat, because I wouldn't make it through this every month without them.

My phone buzzes again, but I don't have the heart to check it. Probably it's Ashe saying that he's either sad for me but hopes I feel better soon, or it's him saying our friendship was a waste of time. Either way, I don't have the energy to look at it, let alone answer. My thirty-minute alarm goes off on my watch, telling me I need to drink some water. I turn it off and take a long gulp from my bottle. Nox isn't pleased that I had to move, but I think, deep down, that her and the alarm are both doing their best at taking care of me. Within a few seconds, I am forgiven, and she resumes her duties as a professional bread baker.

I must have dozed off, because my heavy eyes dart open to strong knocks at the door.

"Mom?" I call out.

But that doesn't make sense. Mom knows the code for the door. She could just come in if she wanted.

Another knock.

"Ugh," I groan as I sit up.

Nox echoes my sentiments with a complimentary grumble.

"I know," I tell her. "And I give you full permission to scratch and hiss if it's an unwelcome solicitor."

Except it's not.

When I open the door, it's not a salesperson or someone with a flier.

It's Ashe. And he's holding a giant grocery bag filled with . . . ice cream?

"Ashe?"

"Hey," he says as he shifts his weight from one foot to another.

He's dressed in baggy gray sweatpants and an oversized black T-shirt. And I'm suddenly very aware that I am in my old pajamas with holes in them because they're my comfort clothes on my heaviest days.

"I got your message," he says. "Can I come in?"

I step aside and close the door behind him. "Sorry for the mess and for, well"—I gesture at myself—"this. I can go change."

He lifts his free hand in front of him. "No, it's okay, I promise. I just came to drop off some things that might help. I hope you don't mind?" He turns and puts the bag on the counter.

116

"I messaged Mira online when you didn't answer, and she said that your favorite ice cream was mint chocolate chip, so I got a tub of that and a few other things."

Tears sting at my eyes and threaten to pour down my face.

"That's really kind," I manage to say. "Thank you."

"For what it's worth, I'm sorry that you're in so much pain."

I give him a sad smile. "You and me both."

Another wave crashes through me and I have to bend over for a few seconds before it passes.

"I think I need to go sit down. Want to join?"

Ashe follows me to the couch and sits in the same spot as he did last time. Nyx doesn't waste any time before snuggling into his side again.

Traitor.

"I'm really sorry," I tell him.

Ashe waves a hand in front of his face. "It's okay, I promise," he says. "Your health is more important than a silly game. Or anything, really."

Again the tears prick at the edges of my eyes. I have to close them to avoid any dramatic waterworks.

"Do you have a comfort film?" Ashe asks.

"What?"

"A comfort film. My aunt used to watch this romantic comedy about some fated mates magic in Rome or something whenever she was on her period. I don't know if it helped her pain or anything, but she seemed more . . . relaxed? Does that make sense?"

I take a deep breath and nod my head.

"So if you could pick anything, what would it be? Can I set it up for you?"

Seriously what is this guy going for, a gold medal in how to be a decent human being? Because if so, he'd win all of

117

them. And I never knew I could be so grateful for such a small act of kindness.

"*Fellowship of the Ring*," I tell him.

He gives me a crooked smile that almost reminds me of my Pops. And now I'm filled with guilt because I forgot to call him. Again.

Tomorrow, I tell myself. Tomorrow is a new day.

"Couldn't have picked better myself."

"It's the first movie on the left—no, your other left," I say after he moves to the wrong side of the TV stand.

I'm half convinced he did it on purpose just to make me laugh.

He opens the case and pops the disc into the DVD player. Thank goodness he's well versed with my system by now. I'm not sure I could manage to switch anything over. Come to think of it, I'm floored by how I even made it to the door in the first place.

The familiar music of the menu plays, and already I'm put more at ease.

"Alright," Ashe says, "there you go. Three hours of uninterrupted magic."

"Four," I groan as I sit up.

"Four?"

"It's the extended edition, obviously."

Ashe lets out a low laugh. "Obviously."

He pats his legs, looks around, and then awkwardly runs his tongue over his teeth. "Okay, well, if there's nothing else I can—"

"Stay?"

The word comes out of my mouth almost on instinct. I feel the heat of embarrassment start to warm my cheeks. "If you want," I add.

Ashe's eyes brighten and a sweet smile plays across his lips.

"Twist my rubber arm."

It takes less than five minutes into the film before I start squirming in my seat. There's just no comfortable place. I'm too hot and too cold at the same time. My skin feels stretched, and there's a thrumming pulsing through my veins that is impossible to ignore.

"Ice cream?" Ashe offers.

I shake my head. "Not yet," I say. "Sorry, just trying to get comfortable."

How were you sitting before I showed up?" he asks.

"I was lying down actually," I admit. "Nox was giving me a massage."

He scoots to the side a bit further and taps his lap. "You can put your feet up if you want. I promise I don't mind."

I don't know what I've done to deserve such a positive karmic reward, but I make a mental note to do an extra special thanks to the universe when I'm properly functional again.

The relief that floods me just from being reclined is enough to make my breath catch.

"Are you okay?"

"Yeah," I breathe. "Much better. Thank you."

Nyx, however, is much less impressed with the new setup. She grumbles as she climbs out from under my legs. I get a spiteful glare before she wanders up onto the lower side of Ashe's lap.

"Someone has a new favorite," I say. "You should be honored."

"To be chosen by a goddess? That's a blessing and a curse. Odysseus would know. And I have no intention of going on that kind of journey."

I giggle. "Don't worry, she won't steal you away. Probably."

Nox jumps up a few moments later and picks up her shift where she left off. Between the happy purrs, the gentle massage, my favorite movie, and my new friend, I find myself in the most relaxed state I've felt all day. My eyes are heavy and I let them fall shut. Maybe if I just rest them for a few moments I'll . . .

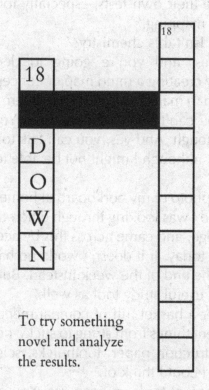

To try something novel and analyze the results.

October 21, 2024

"This test doesn't have any questions on it, teacher," Maggie says as I hand out a blank piece of printer paper to everyone.

"We're going to try something different today," I reply.

"Are we making our own questions?"

"WICKED!"

"Dibs on a question about gas!"

"You would," one student remarks.

"Oh, you must think you're so clever."

"Not this time," I say, interrupting, although I make a mental note of it because it's not a terrible suggestion to have students make their own tests, especially for extra practice. "Today we're mapping."

"Mapping? Isn't this chemistry?"

I nod. "Yes, and you're going to demonstrate your knowledge by creating a mind map or concept map or whatever kind of map makes sense for you. There aren't any rules other than you can't use your textbooks. You can talk with each other, though. And yes, you can talk to me and ask me questions too, although I might not be able to answer everything."

I pull up a photo of my corkboard at home as an example. "This weekend I was looking through different ways to assess your knowledge, and came across this by accident. So we're going to try it today. If it doesn't work, no harm done. We'll do a quiz at the end of the week instead. But if you like it, it might make a useful study tool as well."

I bring over a basket full of compartments containing all sorts of different things from string to sticky-notes, pens, highlighters, construction paper, toothpicks, scissors, glue, and anything else I could think of.

"Here's a box of tools you can use. You can also just use your pencil and paper if you'd rather do that. I won't be grading you on how pretty it looks, but I will be looking at how you organize the information. I suggest planning everything out first and then transferring things onto your final map. Extra paper is here at the front as well," I say as I place the stack of empty white pages onto the table. "You have until the end of the class. Good luck, and I'm looking forward to seeing what you've learned about functional groups."

Some of my students trickle up to the front to look at what they can use. Others stay back and start planning things on their page. A rush of relief sweeps through me when I see Maggie with her head down sectioning things out on the page and making a list of what she wants where. She won't be handing in a blank exam this time.

Even Tobe, who is usually so shy and quiet, has formed a small group of three. When his fellow classmates ask questions, he writes things down, either to help explain or add to the question. I guess I'll find out later. Regardless, I admit it's wonderful to see him interacting with his peers.

The minutes steadily tick by. The majority of my "answers" to students are other questions to help them answer themselves. Sometimes it works and sometimes I need to poke and prod in different ways in order for them to understand. Still, there's nothing like watching a student's eyes light up after they've solved a problem on their own or finally understood something. It always sparks an overwhelming sense of pride in me. I know they can do it. And now they know too.

The bell rings, and everyone places their projects in the tray on the front table. Some of them are extremely colorful, and others are simple and concise. I already know I'm going to love the results of this little experiment. I can only hope that my students do too.

I'm just about to leave for the day when I run into Ashe working on the windows of the doors leading to the parking lot.

"Would you look at this—I'm the one by the door this time."

"Very funny," I say, rolling my eyes, but I can't help the smile that spreads across my face.

Wait, was that supposed to be awkward? It kind of feels awkward. Maybe it's just me?

It's definitely you.

"How are you feeling?" he asks.

I let out a sigh of relief. Not awkward, thank the universe.

"Better," I say. "Thank you. For everything."

I'm granted a warm smile in return. "I'm glad to hear it."

He looks down at the stack of papers in my arms. "Arts and crafts day in chemistry class?"

"Kind of? I'm just trying something out."

He studies me. "Does that have anything to do with the spiderweb of red string on the board in your kitchen?"

I flush and brush a hair behind my ear. "You saw that?" I bite my lip. "Well, that's embarrassing."

The heat rises even further in my face because that was probably the least embarrassing thing I did last weekend. The top contenders probably being a zombie in my Sunday's best attire and falling asleep—and let's be honest, definitely snoring—on Ashe, when all he was trying to do was be a good friend.

"Sorry about, uhm, all of that," I say nervously.

He waves a dismissive hand in front of his face. "Don't be. I thought it was . . . charming?"

Charming? Me? I'm pretty sure I have all the charm of a dry rock in the desert, but I'll take it.

"What was it?" he asks. "Solving a mystery? I'm pretty sure I've only seen red string wrapped around notes like that in movies and true crime documentaries."

"Something like that," I admit. "Assessment strategies."

"Ah." He gives me a knowing nod. "Your homework."

I shrug. "What can I say, I'm a chaotic study."

"I can believe that."

For a moment, neither of us says anything. We're trapped in this spell of quiet . . . something. I can't quite put my finger on it, but it makes my stomach twist and turn.

"Well," Ashe finally says as he moves to face the doors again, "these windows won't wash themselves."

But for some reason, I'm not ready to be finished. With this conversation. With him. With the list. With anything, really. The thought of it gives me a horrible sense of anxiety, which I'm used to feeling when it's the other way around. I realize with a surprise that I sincerely hope I didn't blow it last weekend.

"Ashe?"

He turns around and gazes at me with his dark, round eyes.

"Would you, uhm, want to come with me to Golana this weekend? They're having a two-for-one sale. I figured it might be . . . fun?"

He smirks. "Again with the sales pitch," he teases. "Sure, that sounds great. Saturday?"

I smile back. "Saturday it is."

"It's a date," he says, before returning to the window, leaving me with a warmth in my chest that I'm not sure I'm brave enough to confront.

19 ACROSS

The best form of therapy
is on a printed page.

October 26, 2024

The bell above us rings as I open the door to Golana Books. In many ways, it's my home away from home. The smell immediately takes me, and it feels as if I'm transported into an entirely different realm. I don't know why people don't like reading. Bookstores and books alike have the ability to ground you and send you into a different dimension all at the same time. What's not to love? After all, this world is a mess. I can't imagine anyone not wanting to escape it.

"Make sure you watch the door as it closes," I tell Ashe. "Archie sometimes likes to play the role of escape artist."

Ashe raises an eyebrow at me. "Archie?"

I nod. "The bookstore cat. He should be around here somewhere."

As if on cue, the gorgeous orange tabby comes around the corner to greet us. Every step he takes is accompanied by a high-pitched chirp, as if he is welcoming us himself. Or perhaps lecturing us. Cats are fickle creatures.

Archie rubs against my leg, letting out a long purr, and leaving more than a few hairs behind as a token of our visit. As I bend down to scratch his head, he does a little jump, pushing himself up into my hand, leaning hard into me.

"Archie," I tell the soft baby purring into my palm, "this is Ashe. Ashe, meet Archie, the resident bookstore security man."

Ashe giggles behind me. "Not a very effective security agent," he says, leaning down to let Archie sniff his hand.

"Hmm . . . I disagree. He's quite proficient at stopping people by the door. Even if it is in an unorthodox way."

It takes Archie approximately zero point two seconds to accept Ashe as his new best friend. And within the span of a few breaths, he's putting his paw on Ashe's knee, a sign that he would like to be held like the adorable little baby he is.

"What's this about?" Ashe asks me.

"Just pick him up. I'll show you the rest."

I readjust the orange furball so that he's on his back looking up at Ashe.

"He's a bit heavy," Ashe complains.

"Nonsense," I say in a soft baby voice while scratching Archie's chin. "He's the perfect size. Aren't you, sweetheart?"

Archie lets out another long, deep purr.

"See? He agrees. And it's his house, and his rules."

Ashe laughs at that, and I swear I see something sparkle behind his deep brown eyes. His lips stretch into a wide smile and the skin at his temples crease together. Then he shakes his head slightly at me.

"What?" I ask, returning his smile.

"Nothing, L. Just thinking about how it's nice to see you like this."

"Oh? Like what?"

"Happy."

Happy.

That gives me pause.

Is that what this is? Happiness? I guess so. I feel light, almost at peace. But as soon as I think about it, the persistent nagging returns.

It won't last forever, the gremlins promise. And they're right. It never does. Joy, like everything else good in life, is fleeting.

"Ah, I see you've been catnapped," Sherry says as she comes around the corner.

"A truly terrible fate," Ashe says, sarcastically.

"The worst," Sherry agrees.

The petite woman turns to me, her short brown curls bouncing with every step she takes. She must be at least sixty years old, but in her store, she has the youthfulness of a goddess. I wonder, for a moment, if the secret to immortality is just to simply live and breathe books.

"Anything you're looking for today, L?"

Sherry reaches into the pocket of her white apron and takes a pen and pad of paper out. She must have thousands of requests recorded in it. The pages are yellowed and the spine has been cracked in at least a dozen places. Sherry flips to a new page with ease, as if the small book would rather be wide open for the world to read than be neatly tucked away.

I shake my head from side to side, unsure of whether the answer to that question is yes or no.

"We have more of an idea than anything else," I say.

"Oh?" she asks, intrigued.

"We're going to stay up all night reading," Ashe adds, his arms still full with Archie. He looks like the epitome of contentment, and I'd be lying if I said it didn't make something in my chest soften at the sight.

Sherry beams at us. "Now that's what I call a date!" she exclaims excitedly.

A sudden rush of nerves claims my body.

"Oh—uhm—no . . . that's not—"

"We're just friends, ma'am," Ashe says for both of us. He nods at me, but his eyes fall back down to Archie immediately after they meet mine.

I don't know why, but my stomach turns. Did I eat something bad at lunch? Maybe the weather's changing.

"Ah, well, friends can have dates too you know," Sherry says, still chipper as always. "Let's see what we can hook you two up with. That is how they say it these days, right?"

My whole body is uncomfortably warm and I shift from one foot to the other, trying to ground myself again.

"Sure," I say, because I don't have any idea what she means, but I also don't have the energy to ask and find out either.

"Oh good. We have a new arrival. Care to 'check it out'?" She gives us a knowing side-eye.

I have to admit, it's a great book joke, so I give her as genuine of a laugh as I can manage.

We follow her to the other side of the giant preserved oak tree with a spiral staircase around its trunk that leads to the second floor of the store. There's a cashier desk at the base that has a stack of new releases on it. One of the covers immediately catches my eye. It's so captivating that I find it hard to look at anything else by it.

"Oh yes, we just got a shipment of these in. Isn't the cover amazing?"

The phone on the desk lights up and chimes.

"Sorry, I'll be right back," Sherry says as she moves around to the other side to answer it.

I nod, leaning in to take a closer look at the book in front of me. There are black tentacles that reach up, threatening to devour a ship over a bloodred ocean.

This is dangerous territory for me. I've always been a sucker for a book with a pretty cover.

"L, check this one out," Ashe says beside me, gesturing with his head to a book at the other end of the desk. His arms are still occupied by a sleepy Archie. The cat nuzzles into Ashe's armpit even further and brings his paws over his head to cover his face.

Oh no, another beautiful cover.

The reds, blacks, and golds on the front are extremely striking. Without even reading anything about it, I know it's going to be about a character that kicks ass.

"It was one of my favorite books I read last year. Have you read it?"

I shake my head. "What's it about?"

He thinks for a moment. "Power," he finally says.

"Power?"

"Yes, power. What it means to have it, what it means to grow up without it, what it means to take it, and what people would be willing to do to hold on to it."

I give Ashe a puzzling look.

"What?" he asks me, while absentmindedly stroking Archie between the ears.

"Are you sure you're not a philosophy teacher?" I tease.

He rolls his eyes at me. "Whatever, L. Just read it, okay? I think at the very least you'll appreciate it."

I take the paperback from the stand and trace my thumb over the gold foiled title.

"Okay," I agree. "But on one condition."

Ashe pinches his lips together, pulling the metal ring into his mouth slightly.

"And what's that?"

I lead us over to the start of the fantasy section and look for the C's. My eyes land on it almost immediately.

I pull out the book and hand it to him. "You showed me yours, so now I'm showing you mine." I blush, realizing after the fact how that must have sounded. "My favorite book from last year, that is," I add hastily.

Ashe turns the book over in his hands and reads the blurb on the back.

"Vampires?" he asks, skeptically.

I nod excitedly. "And vampire hunters, and vampire diseases, and a proper love triangle," I say while marking each point on my fingers.

"Finding everything okay?" Sherry asks as she rounds the corner.

Ashe and I look at each other and seemingly come to the same conclusion.

He nods. "It looks like we're swapping favorites tonight."

I line up a row of snacks on my coffee table, complete with chocolate-covered pretzels, gummy candies, an assortment of chip flavors, and a veggie tray because I guess we should have something other than carbohydrates tonight. Or at least look like we will. I make no promises on my end. In fact, I've been eyeing those pretzels since I took them out, and a part of me wants to put them back so I don't have to share them.

We take our seats on my couch and I connect my phone to the TV.

"Any kind of sound I should listen to while reading this?" I ask Ashe.

He readjusts himself so he's sitting with one leg crossed under him, the hem of his black T-shirt draping over his thighs, and then looks at me while squinting his eyes slightly, as if seriously considering my question.

"You have a campfire or fireplace sound on that thing?"

I scroll through the various white noise options and land on a Christmas fire crackling sound.

"Would this work? It's not quite the right season, but I doubt there will be jingle bells in the background."

"Hmm . . . jingle bells would definitely throw me off," he admits. "Okay, but if I hear anything related to metallic chimes, I'm going to blame you for taking me out of the story." Then he looks over at the red book in my hands. "Although, I think it might add something to yours. I guess we'll see what happens."

There's something so intimate about reading. And I don't mean that in the literal physical touchy-feely sense, although there can definitely be parts like that. I mean the ability to leave your body behind and vividly hallucinate parts of a scene to the point where it feels like you are more in the story than out of it. And that's how I find myself thrust into the cockpit of a magic robot, completely disconnected from the world around me. I'm fighting, slashing, stabbing. I'm filled with fire, passion and rage toward this fictional world, because how could they be so cruel to women? What really is the difference between the binary genders? I sure as hell don't understand it in real life, and if anything, this book hammers the point down even further.

I shift and transform into some kind of metal beast, ready to unleash my fury. I punch and kick and scream through a volley of privileged men standing in my way of being who I am meant to be: someone more, someone powerful, someone worth it.

There's a loud rumble that brings me back to my senses, and my eyes flutter open. When did I close them? I'm leaning against something both hard and soft, and there's a warmth to it. A familiar scent of pine fills the air, and it's so comforting that I lean into it more. No, not it. *Him.*

Suddenly I am very aware that I'm nuzzled into Ashe, who must have fallen asleep beside me as well. There's a low rumble from him that sounds like a distant roll of thunder, and the rhythmic rise and fall of his chest is so peaceful that it threatens to lull me back under. It's dark outside, definitely long past my bedtime, so I finally just relax and let sleep take me again. The last thing I see before I close my eyes again is that my book isn't in my lap or hands anymore. It's on the coffee table with my Archie bookmark poking out from the pages. My glasses sit gently folded on top. I don't have the energy to wonder how they got there or who put them there before sleep finally pulls me under once again.

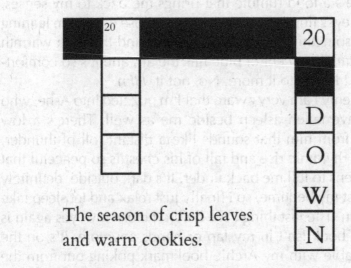

The season of crisp leaves
and warm cookies.

October 27, 2024

I wake up to the smell of fresh coffee and something that smells like cinnamon sugar. Oh fuck, am I drooling? I hate drooling. What is that smell? Did I leave a candle on or something? And I don't remember setting up the coffee pot last night.

Last night.

Oh dear Universe.

I bolt up on the couch and look into the kitchen. Ashe has his hair pulled back and my "FEMME IN STEM" apron on over his clothes.

He peers at me over the lip of his mug. "Good morning," he says, his voice husky from disuse.

"Morning."

I brush my fingers through my hair only to get stuck immediately in a tangle. Damn curls. I grab a hair tie from my water bottle and quickly wrap my hair up into a bun on the top of my head. There. Much better.

I'm still in my clothes from yesterday, which feel all wrong on my body this morning. Mornings are meant for showers and fresh clothes. THEN coffee and . . . cookies?

I stand up and make my way over to the kitchen to find a plate of still-warm snickerdoodles sitting on the kitchen counter.

"I'm glad I didn't wake you up. And well, you loved these so much, I figured I'd make some fresh. I hope that's okay."

I throw my morning routine out the proverbial window and stuff my face with the little slice of heaven on a plate. I can't help the moan that comes from my chest as the sugar hits my tongue.

A muscle tenses in Ashe's jaw and he takes another sip of coffee.

"Fuck," I say, tilting my head and rolling my eyes back in my head for dramatic effect. I finish chewing before saying anything else though, because there is absolutely no way I am wasting a single moment with this cookie. "More than okay," I reassure him. "This is the best wakeup I've had in a long time."

Nox rubs up against my leg and paws at my foot.

"Good morning to you too, little goddess," I say while I lean down and give her head a few pats. And, as always, this prompts Nyx to join the party.

"Breakfast?"

The two of them meow at me excitedly as I make my way to the pantry and take out two packages of wet food for them.

"Someone's spoiled," Ashe comments.

"As they should be," I retort.

I add three treats to the top of their meals before letting them dive in. After I wash my hands, I make sure to pour myself a coffee and take another cookie.

"For the record, I'm spoiled too. Thank you," I say.

"Oh, I'm sorry," he says with just a hint of something playful in his voice. "That is what I meant."

I nudge him with my shoulder gently. "Very funny."

"I know."

We watch the twins finish their breakfast in a comfortable silence. A few moments later, Ashe's alarm softly plays on his phone. He grabs the oven mitts from the counter and opens the oven, letting the hot air rise out for a bit before leaning in and grabbing the fresh tray of cookies.

My eyes wander as he squats down, and I mentally scold myself. What am I? Some hormonal teenager? Stupid morning brain.

"Hot and ready," he says as he puts the tray on the stovetop.

I can feel my gremlins raise an intrigued eyebrow.

I need a cold shower. Like right now.

"I would you like to go shower?" I ask, and immediately flush. Somehow instead of telling him that I would like to go shower, my brain also thought about offering him a shower and well . . . let's just say that the wires aren't just crossed— this is a more of tangled mess.

Ashe turns to look at me over his shoulder.

I shake my head. "Sorry. What I meant to say was that I'm feeling a bit, uhm, grimy? And I think I'm going to go shower."

He shrugs. "Okay."

I quickly drink the rest of my coffee and race to the bathroom. My reflection is a startled mess of stray hairs and red blotches on my face. I sigh and turn on the tap to cold.

Ice cold.

I'm feeling somewhat more composed when I come back out. Ashe has two bowls in front of him, one full of a white cookie dough, and the other with what looks like some kind of sparkly brown dust.

"Want to help?" he asks.

I wash my hands at the sink and stand beside him.

"What can I do?"

"Here, watch me," he says as he dunks the dough in the dust, rolls it around with some spoons, and then places it on the cookie sheet.

"It's tedious, but they always taste so much better this way than if we just put the cinnamon sugar on top."

Oh, so that's what it is. I briefly wonder what it would taste like on its own, but reconsider. I mean, what would Ashe think if he just saw me dunk my finger in it? Then again, do I care what he thinks?

"Does that make sense?" he asks, breaking my train of thought.

I nod.

I'm slow at first, but it gets easier with each cookie.

"You're really good at this, you know," I tell him.

"At baking cookies? I'd hope so. I did spend a good chunk of my early adult years in a bakery, after all."

I shake my head as I roll the next drop of dough. "No, at this. Taking care of people. Being kind."

Ashe lets out a nervous laugh. "Yeah, I guess that comes with practice too," he says before letting out a long sigh.

I sprinkle some extra cinnamon sugar on the top of the cookie after placing it on the tray.

"Sounds like there's a story there."

He takes a deep breath and raises his shoulders. "Yes and no. Long story short, I had to get good at reading signs because, well, if I didn't . . . let's just say it wasn't pleasant."

His posture has changed and I feel horrible for bringing up what is obviously a painful subject.

"I'm sorry," I say, because there isn't really anything else to say.

"Thanks," he breathes. Then he straightens slightly. "Took a few years of therapy to realize that I wasn't the problem of everything in my life. Did you know that people are not naturally mind readers?"

At least his tone is somewhat back to the teasing Ashe that I know.

"Could have fooled me," I said lightheartedly.

"Oh, I fooled quite a lot of people . . . for a long time," he confesses. "Right up until . . . it almost killed me."

I stop rolling. Ashe has stopped as well. He's looking at me as if trying to decide something.

"Literally?" I ask quietly, unsure of whether I want to know the answer.

"Close enough," he says, soft eyes still trained on mine. "I didn't realize how much of myself I had lost until . . ."

Ashe runs a hand through his hair, leaving a streak of cinnamon sugar in his dark curls. He looks down at his hand.

"You think I'd learn," he says, scolding himself.

He makes his way to the sink and washes his hand and then brushes his fingers through his hair.

"Here, let me," I say, dunking my hand under the warm water.

I gently stroke through until everything is out.

"Thanks," he says.

"You know," I tell him. "It's okay to let people help you too."

He lets out a low laugh, and I offer him a towel to dry his hands and hair.

"Yeah." There's a hint of hesitation in his voice. "Still trying to learn that, I guess."

"Me too," I admit as I raise a shoulder. "But you can't be there to help everyone else if you don't help yourself first."

He gives me a soft smile. "Careful, you almost sound like a therapist."

I lean back against the counter. "Well, it's probably Iris talking through my lips right now anyway."

"They have a habit of doing that."

We both giggle at his comment.

"Can I ask you something?"

He thinks for a second and then finally nods.

"What part of yourself did you hold on to the most?"

Ashe looks surprised at my question.

"Before, you said you had lost a lot of yourself. So, what did you hold on to?"

His throat works as he swallows. "I"—he cuts himself off and shakes his head. "You . . . already know, I think." His head is low and he looks up at me through thick lashes like a puppy afraid of what might come next.

Ashe runs his tongue through the seam of his lips. His cinnamon-coated fingers fiddle at the sides of the apron, leaving faint streaks behind.

"That night at trivia was the first night I had been myself in a long time. I'd forgotten what it was like to just exist completely, and you coaxed that out of me. I hadn't felt that free in years. My ex-girlfriend was always telling me that I spent too much time watching 'those stupid cartoons' and playing 'those stupid games,' but you didn't think it was stupid at all. It was like . . . I don't know."

"A breath of fresh air?" I offer.

He nods. "Yeah, something like that."

I can't imagine being stuck in a relationship where I felt so trapped that I couldn't even enjoy the things I love.

Isn't that what you do to yourself?

Iris' voice in my head catches me off guard. It's not the same as Ashe's situation, but whatever that thought came from is right. I have been stopping myself. But not because I needed to put someone else first. It's because I was always scared of what might come after. The thought is humbling in a way that I never expected.

"I'm sorry she didn't take the time to understand you," I tell him. It's almost like an apology to myself in a way as well.

"Thanks," he says. "It's over now, obviously. And I moved here a few months later to hopefully start fresh in a place where no one had any assumptions or expectations of me."

A sudden pang of guilt hits me.

"Oh, I'm so sorry. Last weekend, you came over and . . . oh, Ashe, I didn't mean to put that pressure on you."

His brows furrow. "Pressure?" he asks.

"I sent you that text about feeling miserable, and then you showed up to help. I didn't mean to force you to come take care—"

"That was different," he interrupts.

I'm shocked by his sudden change in tone.

"That was different," he says again, softer this time. "I wanted to. You didn't pressure me, L. I promise. I wanted to come." Ashe's fingers fiddle with the fabric of the apron. "And I'd do it again." A muscle in his jaw tenses and he swallows before one side of his mouth tilts up in a crooked smile. His dimples seem to wink at me. "That's what friends do."

His gaze is firmly fixed on mine, pinning me in place. I don't know what to say to that.

"Thank you," is the only thing that sounds appropriate, and yet it is so short of how I actually feel.

E. A. M. Trofimenkoff

Ashe turns back around and continues working on his dough rolls. I sprinkle a few before finally cutting the silence again.

"Ashe," I say, unsure of how to properly phrase my question.

He tilts his head to look at me with curious, wide eyes.

"I know that you like helping people. I mean, that's pretty obvious. But . . ." I run my teeth over my lower lip. "Who takes care of you when you need it?"

Ashe freezes and sucks in a shuddering breath as if I had punched him straight in the gut. The color drains from his face, and his focus wanders, as if his mind has taken him somewhere far from here.

Shit, I completely miscalculated this.

Small pools of glistening tears begin to form at the corners of his eyes.

"I'm sorry," he says as he turns his head away. He wipes at his face with the back of his hand.

I give his shoulder a reassuring squeeze.

"No, I'm sorry," I tell him. "I didn't mean to pry."

Ashe shakes his head and holds on to the edge of the counter as if trying to steady himself. He looks down at the floured surface and the muscles in his jaw flex as he clenches his teeth.

"My nan," he finally says. "My parents left me with her when I was a baby . . . She was . . . the last one . . . to care." He looks around the counter at the ridiculous number of cookies we have prepared. "And these"—he holds out a dough roll in his palm—"were her favorite."

A small tear begins to course down his face.

"Oh, Ashe."

I wrap my arms around his soft body and pull his head into the crook of my neck. He lets out a series of shaky breaths before holding me back.

"She must have been a remarkable woman," I tell him, "to raise such a compassionate grandson. What a gift she gave you."

He nods his head in my shoulder.

"She was," he whispers.

I give him another tight squeeze.

"I'm sorry," he says again as he pulls away.

I hand him some paper towel from the corner of the counter, and he gratefully accepts it.

"For being human?" I shake my head. "No, Ashe. You have nothing to apologize for."

He blows his nose and throws out the paper towel.

"Then I guess I should say thank you," he says after taking a few steadying breaths. "For giving me the space to show myself. And for not judging what you see."

I give him a warm smile and move back to the cookies.

"You are welcome, Ashe. There is room for every part of you here. Always."

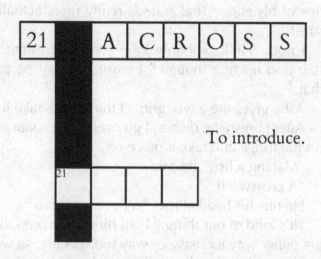

21 ACROSS

To introduce.

October 27, 2024

"What are we going to do with all these cookies?" Ashe asks as his eyes sweep the full countertop.

I'm scrubbing at one of the bowls when a thought occurs to me.

"Do you have plans today?" I ask.

He shakes his head. "No, why?"

I run my tongue over my teeth. "How are you with seniors?"

Ashe studies me curiously.

"Grade twelve students? I don't know," he says as he runs a hand through his hair. "Fine, I guess?"

I bite my lips together to stop a giggle. "No, not high school students—seniors as in age. How would you feel about meeting my Pops?"

I've told Ashe about him a few times, and it feels so natural to think about introducing them. If I'm being honest with myself, I'm actually excited about the idea.

"Oh." A light blush blooms across his cheekbones to the tips of his ears. "That sounds really nice, actually. Are you sure?"

I nod. "He'll probably give you a hard time about your hair and lip ring though," I warn, "so just be prepared for that."

Ashe gives me a wry grin. "I think I can take it."

After I finish the dishes, I go over to the spare pad of paper on the fridge and take a piece off.

"Making a list?" he asks.

"A crossword."

He tilts his head at me. "A . . . crossword?"

"It's kind of our thing," I tell him. "The ones in the papers are either way too easy or way too specific, so we make our own now. It's actually really fun. Want to try?"

Ashe continues drying the dishes and pinches his lips to the side.

"I think I'll let you have the fun this time around," he says.

I shrug. "Suit yourself."

So, naturally, a few minutes later, after he's used my spare toothbrush and rinsed off in the shower himself, Ashe is looking over my shoulder giving me suggestions on what words to use and what prompts to give.

"Oh, I know," he says. "How about 'brown ones don't make chocolate milk.'"

I look up at him and raise a brow.

"What? It's one of the first things I learned after moving here."

I scoff. "You didn't really think that chocolate milk came from brown cows, did you?"

"No," he says, dryly, "but I did learn that some people do."

I roll my eyes. "Okay, three down is 'cow.' What next?"

We go back and forth for the better part of an hour before we finally have a semi-decently constructed puzzle.

"Alright," I say, folding the paper and tucking it into my pocket. "Let's go see if Pops knows how chocolate milk is made."

Ashe carefully balances three stacked containers full of cookies as he holds the door for me.

"Thanks."

I hold the next door for him in return. When we're both through, I make sure to sign our names on the guest form at the front desk.

"I always forget to do this," I admit. "I'm usually too focused on visiting. Plus, everyone knows me anyway."

"Right, small town."

"Don't I know it."

We make our way through the halls until we arrive at door 103. I give my classic tap-tap-ta-tap-tap . . . tap-tap knock.

"Pops?" I say as I open the door. "It's L, and I brought a friend with me too."

Pops doesn't miss a beat. "Well don't loiter in the hall," he calls from what sounds like the living room. "They have rules about that, you know."

I hold the door for Ashe and he squeezes into the apartment beside me.

After a few steps, we're in the open living area.

Pops is still hooked up to oxygen. He has been ever since he came back. But he has some more color to his face today, which is good to see.

"Pops, I'd like you to meet Ashe." I turn to Ashe and take the cookies from his arms. "Ashe, this is my Pops."

"Nice to meet you, sir," Ashe says as he shakes Pops' hand.

"Sir?" Pops looks around Ashe to raise an eyebrow at me. "I didn't realize I was being knighted by the queen."

"Sorry I forgot my sword," Ashe says without missing a beat.

Pops' eyes flash with amusement and he winks at me. "I knew I'd like you," he says, gesturing for Ashe to sit next to him.

Ashe accepts the recliner and adjusts the bottom of his shirt before sitting down and crossing his legs.

"So, L tells me you work at the high school with them."

"Yes, I'm one of the new custodians."

Pops nods and makes an approving grumble. "So what you're saying is that you keep the school functional so that L has somewhere to teach."

Ashe laughs. "Not that extreme. Although, there would surely be a gum wall without me."

"And what a sticky situation that would be," Pops chides back, resulting in a series of giggles from both of us.

I take the lid off the cookies so they don't build up any condensation, and bring a container over for us.

"Ooh," Pops says, following me with his eyes. "And what do we have today?"

"Snickerdoodles," I tell him.

"They were my nan's favorite," Ashe adds. It fills my chest with a warmth I have only experienced on a few occasions. Immediately I know the word for it: joy.

"Her recipe?" Pops asks as he takes a cookie and turns it over in his hand.

"Of course."

I move over a chair from the small card table in the corner to sit with them.

"Any . . . secret ingredient I should know about?"

Ashe shakes his head. "Only a secret technique," he says.

"Oh?"

"I believe the recipe card says, and I quote, 'whip the shit out of the butter, sugar, and eggs, you coward.'"

That sends us all into a fit of laughter.

"A woman to be reckoned with. I like that," Pops says.

"Especially in the kitchen," Ashe says. "That's why I got into baking. I was afraid if my skills weren't up to her standards that she might never teach me how to make her famous cookies."

"A frightful thought indeed," Pops agrees. "These are spectacular!"

"Thank you," Ashe says. A light pink dusts his cheeks.

Pops readjusts himself slightly so he can see me better. "And how's my favorite grandkid?"

I roll my eyes. "I'm your only grandkid."

"Well, then it's a good thing you're my favorite. But watch out—this one might take your place if you're not careful."

Ashe and I exchange a glance, and the warmth in my chest blooms. For the first time in a long time, I don't stop it.

"I like a bit of competition," I admit.

"You get that fighting spirit from me," Pops says.

I nod. "Undoubtedly."

He takes another cookie and eats it in two bites. "And how were classes this week? Did your experiment turn out?"

"Yes, actually," I say between bites. "I was inspired by my murder board, as you like to call it."

"You still have that thing?"

"Who else is going to solve crimes and save the world?" Ashe says, giving me a playful grin.

"I've been saying that since they were a kid."

"You two give me too much credit," I tell them.

Pops shakes his head. "No, I don't think so. You give yourself too little."

I drop my gaze to my black running shoes.

Ashe's voice dissipates the clouds beginning to swirl in my brain. "I think I'd have to agree with you on that one, Pops. I can call you Pops, right?"

"Of course! You are my favorite grandkid, after all."

That gets my attention.

"Hey!" I say.

Everyone breaks out into laughter again.

When we've caught our breath, Pops reaches out his hand.

"You have a puzzle for me?"

I retrieve the folded paper from my jacket and place it in his open palm.

"Ashe," Pops says, "can you reach into the side pocket there and grab mine?"

Ashe leans over and takes out a small paper crane. I look back at Pops questioningly.

"What? I was bored. And it was a rec activity for us old folks. Can't I learn something new?"

I roll it over in my hand. "I don't really want to unfold it," I admit.

"That's okay," he says. "You can always do it later."

We sit in silence as Pops works through the puzzle.

Then Ashe moves his hands in a circle toward himself. If I didn't know any better, I would think that he was trying to summon me over to him in an awkward middle grade dance type of way. Except I do know better. It's sign language. And he's asking if I want to practice.

"What's that secret message stuff about?" Pops asks.

I giggle. "It's not a secret message, Pops. It's sign language. Ashe is teaching me."

Pops looks up from his paper. "And so the teacher becomes the student once again."

I shrug. "Something like that," I admit. "One of my students communicates easier through ASL, so I figured I would learn some."

Ashe and Pops share a look.

"Like I said," Pops says under his breath as he goes back to his crossword, "not enough credit."

I take a long breath and sit back in my chair. Together, Ashe and I work through the alphabet three full times. He also teaches me the signs for paper, pen, yes, and no, which I catch on to pretty easily.

"Aha!"

Ashe and I both look over to Pops.

"Finished," he says as he puts his pen down. "A few challenges in there, L." He waves a finger at me. "But I saw through them, don't you worry."

"I never doubted you for a second."

"Good." He turns to Ashe. "Now, tell me, are you from around here?"

And so the line of questioning begins. I thought Pops might lead with that, but then again, he does like to get people comfortable and throw them off their game, so maybe I shouldn't be so surprised.

"Kind of," Ashe says. "I was born and raised in Calgary."

"Ah, a city boy. That explains the lip ring and the funky haircut."

There it is.

"I guess so."

They continue back and forth for several rounds. Somehow, Ashe doesn't look offended or taken aback by any of the questions that Pops throws his way. I'm not surprised. I somehow knew that they would get along.

"One last thing," Pops says as he sits up straighter. He looks at me and then back at Ashe.

"As you know, my L here is nonbinary. I am very protective of them. So, I must know, are you an ally, or do I need to kick you out of my apartment and out of my will?"

Ashe smiles.

"I'm a part of the community too, Pops, so no need to worry. I see L for who they are. And who they are is"—Ashe locks eyes with me—"really freaking special."

My breath catches in my throat and I flex my jaw to keep from letting out a choking sound.

"I couldn't agree more."

With a strong push, Pops stands from his chair and motions for us to give him a hug.

"Come on in, kids. Give this old man a hug and then go do something careless and exciting so you can tell me all about it."

I give him a strong squeeze. "I love you, Pops."

"I love you too, kid."

After wrapping Ashe in probably the biggest bear hug I think I've ever seen him give, Pops walks us both to the door, wheeling his oxygen behind him.

"You can give the rest of the cookies to the other residents if you like," I tell him as I rotate the handle.

"Pssh, as if I would share."

We all laugh at that.

"Fair point," Ashe says.

"Oh, one more thing before you go," Pops calls.

I turn back around to find him scratching his head.

"Who the hell thinks that brown cows make chocolate milk?"

A substance used to decorate.

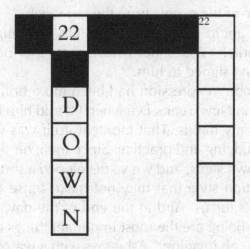

November 10, 2024

My body still aches from laser tag. It's been a week, and my muscles continue to protest. Or maybe that's from the trampoline park I went to with Mira, Jo and Vic the next day. Or the impromptu coulee hike I did a few nights ago. Regardless, my body hurts, but it did mean I was able to cross off three things from my list: laser tag, trampoline, nature walk. There are only a few things left, and a part of me is disappointed that it's almost finished.

At this point, it feels more like a lifestyle than a chore or a therapy assignment. And it's given me a chance to form a new friendship that I can't imagine my life without now. If Ashe and I don't see each other at school, we find ourselves at a park or a cafe, sometimes discussing the list, but mostly talking about life. Barely a day goes by where we don't at least send each other a meme we don't understand, but know the other will. It's a kind of low-pressure love language between the two of us that feels foreign and familiar all at the same time.

As we make our way to my bathroom, I fill Ashe in on some of the events from the last week.

"I got to use some of the signs you taught me," I tell him, proudly. "You should have seen the look on Tobe's face when I signed to him."

Tobe's expression had been more brilliant than the night sky on New Year's Eve when I'd told him he was smart using only my hands. That moment itself was worth all the hours of studying and practice. Since then, he's taught me a few of his own signs, and we've developed a sort of hybrid communication style that may not make sense to everyone, but it works for us. And at the end of the day, his education and well-being are the most important things anyway.

"I can imagine," Ashe says with a warm smile. "You catch on quickly."

I tilt my head from side to side. "Well, I guess practice and good teaching makes a difference after all."

"Still thinking about taking the course next semester?" he asks.

I nod. "I think so."

As it turned out, even with Silva's recommendation, I couldn't get in the class this term. Fortunately I have a skilled private tutor.

"Good," he says. "It's better to learn from a deaf instructor if you can."

When we finally make it to the bathroom, Ashe gives me an awkward glance.

"What's the . . . I don't know . . . protocol here?" Ashe asks. His gaze darts between me, with the bag of painting supplies in my arms and the marble-white bathtub.

E. A. M. Trofimenkoff

"Protocol?"

He nods and shifts his weight to his right leg, placing his hands in his jean pockets.

"Are you asking me if there are rules to finger painting in a bathtub? Because I'm pretty sure the only rule is 'don't eat the paint.'"

He hums thoughtfully. "And you're sure it's just going to . . . wash off?"

I pull out the small jugs of paint from the bag and show them to him.

"Look, see here?" I turn over the bottle in my hand. "Washable paint. It will be fine! What's the worst that could happen?"

Ashe cocks an eyebrow at me. "I could come out of there looking like a unicorn threw up on me."

"Nah, I didn't pick up pea green for that reason," I tease. "It's not your color."

I carefully line up the bottles on the edge of the tub and place a few towels on the floor just outside of it to catch any spills. Then I grab the bottom of my shirt and pull it over my head. I wore my painting bra for just this reason. The air of the bathroom is cold against my skin, and it sends goose-bumps along my skin. I shiver thinking about how the tub is only going to make it colder.

"L."

I turn around and see Ashe looking like a statue, eyes fixed on some point behind me.

"What are you doing?" he asks. A muscle ticks in his jaw, and he still won't make eye contact with me.

"Getting ready to tub paint?" I have no idea what he's getting at. What does it look like I'm doing?

He finally meets my gaze, and his face flushes. "What?" he asks.

153

"You're just standing there like you're in pain. Are you okay?"

He swallows and takes his eyes away from me again. "I'm fine."

I don't believe him for a second. Ashe's shoulders hunch forward slightly and I can see him fidgeting his fingers in his pocket. He's . . . nervous?

"You don't have to mask for me," I finally say. "I can tell you're uncomfortable. Did I do something?"

I take a step toward him and am relieved when he doesn't flinch or take a step back.

Ashe shakes his head, takes a deep breath and looks up at the ceiling.

"No, it's . . . it's just . . . I . . . CanIleavemyshirton?"

I think my brain has misfired because not a single syllable of his sentence properly registers.

"I'm sorry?"

"My shirt . . . can I . . . keep it on?"

"Oh my god," I say, embarrassed. Did he think I was trying to seduce him in the bathtub? "Yes, yes of course! Please, you're allowed to be comfortable. I mean, obviously you should be comfortable. And, I mean, the tub might be a bit cold anyway so it's probably a good idea to have a layer between you and the porcelain." And now that the rambles have begun, there is no stopping them. "You don't have to— I just don't want paint on mine. And I always do painting projects like this." I am suddenly very aware that there is only the thin lining of my lime green sports bra keeping my breasts from being on full display. And it's cold in here which means . . . yup, they're perky. Yikes. "And I'm sorry if it felt like I was . . . uhm . . . pressuring you? I swear I'm not trying to seduce you."

Smooth.

Ashe's eyes widen in surprise.

Fuck. That's not the response I was expecting.

"You . . . didn't think I was trying to seduce you . . . did you?" I ask, sheepishly.

He lets out an awkward laugh. "No . . . I didn't."

I bite my lip and try to keep my feet firmly planted on the ground so I don't run away and never come back.

"So, uh, is it a religious thing?" I ask. "The shirt, I mean."

"Oh, no," he says, looking down and fiddling with the bottom hem. "It's a . . . me thing."

Everything finally clicks.

"Yeah," he says, acknowledging the look that must be on my face. "I'm not super comfortable showing my skin. It's . . . I have a lot of stretch marks. And when I'm cold they get really red and my skin gets all blotchy so . . . if it's okay . . . can I keep my shirt on?"

Something catches in my throat and I have to force myself not to cry. I remember that feeling all too well. All I want to do is hold him and tell him that everything is going to be okay and that he's perfect the way he is and that there's nothing wrong with his body. Because that's what I needed someone to tell me all those years ago.

"Can I give you a hug?" I ask him.

"What?" he asks, surprised.

I hold out my arms to him and take a tentative step forward. "Can I hug you?"

A thin shiny layer of tears begins to well at the sides of his eyes. Then he gives me a nod and closes the space between us.

Ashe isn't much taller than I am, so I rest my chin on his shoulder and lean my head against his. I wrap one arm around his back and the other around his neck, and twist the ends of his hair in my fingers.

155

"You don't have to try to fit your skin, Ashe. You can just exist, and that's more than enough. And for what it's worth, I think your body is just right."

He breathes out a low laugh. "Thanks, Goldilocks."

The tub is definitely a tight fit for the two of us. Our legs tangle together in awkward angles, and there's not a lot of room to paint, since the tub is mostly filled with our bodies.

I start mixing colors to see if I can come up with various shades of green for my forest scene I have planned. I finally find a combination that's close to the color of fresh buds on trees in spring.

"You know how usually blue is the color for boys and pink for girls? I think if I had to choose a color for my gender, it would be this one."

Ashe looks over and gives me a supportive nod. "I can see that," he says. "It suits you."

To my surprise, he doesn't resume painting.

"What?" I ask. His stare is gentle and forceful all at the same time.

"How did you know you were nonbinary?" Ashe asks. There's genuine curiosity behind his expression. And if I'm being honest, I appreciate the forwardness of the question. I'm tired of having conversations with people who dance around what they really mean.

I shrug. "How do you know you're a man?"

Ashe looks down and rubs a blob of red into his drop of blue. It turns into a muddy purple and he wrinkles his nose at it.

"I don't know," he admits. "I've never really thought about it."

"Well, you have some time now. Take a few minutes."

I continue working on my forest scene while Ashe absent-mindedly runs his fingers through the paint on his side of the tub. My heart warms knowing that he's actually taking this seriously.

"There's no list," he mumbles.

"List?" I ask.

He nods. "Like, there's no prescription. Something that I can use as a guide? Does that make sense?"

I chuckle. "More than you know."

"Hmm . . ." he grumbles.

"You're thinking about boobs and testicles, aren't you?"

Ashe flicks a bit of red paint at me, but he can't wipe the soft smile on his face.

"What? It's what everyone eventually gets to. Hell, it's what I used to think about all the time too. So to take you through my checklist, no, you don't need boobs to be a woman—breast cancer survivors tell us that much. And no, you don't need ovaries to be a woman either, because there are plenty of cases where women are born with undescended testes. Or what if they have PCOS and need to have their ovaries removed, or what about the women who have hysterectomies? Or menopausal women?" I pause to take a breath because as much as I would love to sit here and discuss every single case, the reality is that it doesn't matter.

"That's a lot to consider," Ashe agrees.

"Yup."

I add a few hints of blue around my trees. "Even though I identify as a femme, I don't feel like a woman. The label never fit. But nonbinary feels . . . like that tingling sensation when you step out into the sun. It's right. It's as natural as breathing to me. What I realized is that genitalia doesn't matter. Chromosomes don't matter either. So what is it? What's the deciding factor? Or is there even one? And I guess my biggest question is, why does it matter in the first place? What does having these classifiers even give us? Other than up-holding archaic patriarchal systems."

Ashe laughs this time. "Damn, L," he says, "you should have been a philosopher."

I sigh. "I know. I spend a lot of my time thinking about things. I feel like a four-year-old, perpetually in their 'why' stage."

"Maybe you should write a book," he suggests.

I scoff. *"L's Rambles: How to be a Decent Human Being in a Hundred Thousand Words or Less."*

"Rolls right off the tongue," he teases.

"I feel like it would come off as more of a cult text."

"I'd join that cult, I think."

"You say that now," I jest. "Who or what would we even worship? Me?"

"Would that be such a bad thing?"

Ashe's gaze meets mine, and suddenly my mouth goes dry. He didn't mean . . . surely he wasn't insinuating—

"I think you'd make a great leader, L. I mean, you prove it every day. Those kids are really lucky to have you. I wish I had a teacher who really thought things through when I was in high school."

Duh, I mentally scold myself. *Get your head out of the gutter, weirdo.*

"Are you saying my classroom is a cult meeting, Ashe?" I joke, still trying to get myself out of whatever that weird headspace was.

"Oh most definitely." His tone drips of sarcasm, and he smiles so wide that his dimples show on his cheeks. "I can't imagine a more corrupting institution."

I roll my eyes. "Shut up and paint your flowers," I say, flicking specks of blue paint at him.

He laughs and resumes his work.

It doesn't take long until we've exhausted the available space in the tub.

"Well, what do you think?" I ask, proudly displaying my forest scene.

"I think you try very hard to be the best at everything you do," he says without hesitating. "And this is no different."

I raise my chin. "Does that mean I've won at tub painting?" I tease.

Ashe looks over to his flowers. "I don't think I ever stood a chance," he says, shaking his head.

He turns back to me. There's a playful sparkle in his eyes. "What do we do to clean up?"

I point to the wall behind him. "There's a shower dial behind you. We can get out and just use some water to wipe down the tub. As for us"—I gesture to our now colorful clothes—"this should just come out in the wash. No problem."

Ashe nods, braces his arms on the sides of the bathtub, and pushes himself out.

There's a small click and then ice-cold water begins shooting directly at me from the showerhead.

Instinctively I put my hands up in front of my face to protect myself from the sudden onslaught. And while that might have been a good decision in a normal situation, in addition to the freezing water, I am rewarded with several layers of dirt-tasting paint in my mouth as I try to gurgle out, "Turn it off!"

"Shit!"

I can hear Ashe fiddling with the lever, but there's no change in the temperature or the force of the water which has now completely drenched me.

Stupid tap. I should have gotten it fixed months ago. But here we are. If it isn't the consequences of my own actions.

I sit forward and reach my hand out. The rivers of water coursing down my lenses have completely clouded my vision. I can barely make out Ashe, who is squatting at the edge, trying to push the lever back and forth to no avail. When I reach the tub spout, I pull up the metal diverter. Immediately the water switches from the showerhead to the spout, giving me a moment of reprieve to gather myself.

Unfortunately that moment is short-lived. Within a second, Ashe slips on the slick bottom. His feet catch mine and I land on top of him, hand draped over his stomach, legs straddling one of his own.

"Ugh," I groan as my other arm braces against the cold porcelain.

"Sorry," Ashe grunts as he tries to push himself up.

With one final reach, I twist the dial to turn off the icy onslaught. I wipe off my glasses as best as I can with my bra.

"Are you okay?" I ask.

He nods.

A silence stretches between us as we both register the situation we're in: me on top of him, and him stretched out as if enjoying a good show.

Neither one of us is able to look away. Despite the cold water, there is a scorching heat flooding my veins, threatening to overflow and bubble up. A light pink blooms in Ashe's cheeks as he looks up at me, and I can't help but think that there is an innocent beauty in him that I have never seen before. It's like the start of an idea that has been nagging at my brain for months and has finally risen to the surface. He's so close. If I wanted to, I could just reach out, soothe the flush in his cheeks and feel how warm his lips—

"Sorry," Ashe says again before clearing his throat.

I shake my head, trying to clear my mind. What was I thinking?

"No, it's okay," I tell him as I push myself up. I can't help but feel the missing space where his body used to press against mine.

"I thought I had enough space to stand. Clearly not."

The pink has transformed to a dusty red all over his face and the tips of his ears. His eyes turn down to the tub and he bites at the inside of his cheek.

Is he . . . embarrassed?

"Ashe," I say leaning over and offering him a hand, "it's okay. I promise."

He lets out a long sigh and accepts my hand. I help him to his feet and can't help the giggle that escapes from my chest.

His gaze lightens, and within seconds the two of us are in stitches from laughter. It's been ages since I laughed like this. My stomach hurts, I can't breathe, tears leak from my eyes, and despite everything, I can't stop. I don't want to.

When I finally catch my breath, I look up into his beautiful brown eyes.

"What?" he asks, a smile still stretched over his lips.

I shake my head. "My friends are never going to believe this."

"What a day," I say to Nyx and Nox as I climb into bed.

The twins snuggle into each other at the end of the blanket, transforming into a single black void.

I lie on my back with my hands behind my head staring at the ceiling, and begin my nightly playthrough of L's best hits. Images of myself at a young age not sharing my swing, speaking out of turn, and doubling down on a rude comment because I was too embarrassed to admit my wrongs frequent

my mind. Within minutes, I'm exhausted, but not even re-
motely sleepy. I roll over onto my side and try to think about
anything else.

Come on, stupid brain. Give me something nice.

Sorry, it responds, *best I can do is crippling guilt.*

I groan and roll over again. There's a pent-up energy
coursing through me that makes me feel like I either need to
go run a marathon, lift a car, or . . .

I look over at Stanley, my trusty best friend, on my night
table.

"Worth a try," I say to myself as I grab the black vibrator
and push it under my shorts. Then I turn on my spicy audio-
book, select my favorite chapter, and hope my brain finally
decides to focus on something else.

"You're a five-course meal worth devouring," the male
voice-actor says in a low, gravelly voice.

Yup, that'll do it.

I close my eyes and let the scene envelop me. I imagine
the characters taking their turns with me, one working me
with their fingers while the other makes slow gentle sucks on
my clit . . . just like Stanley does. I wonder if that's what
Ashe's tongue would—

No.

I interrupt the thought immediately.

No getting distracted.

Back to Stanley. He's so good at his job.

Yes. Head in the game.

Clit suction vibrators are severely underrated.

"So wet for me."

I suck in a breath, and I don't stop the moan that falls from
my lips.

The faceless figure drapes himself over me, kissing my
neck, running his tongue over my collarbone and around my
nipples.

E. A. M. Trofimenkoff

I arch up as a wave of heat courses through me.

So close now. So close.

Suddenly the faceless, shapeless form isn't indistinguishable anymore. The subject of my fantasy isn't a stranger. Quite the opposite. I would know those gorgeous brown eyes anywhere. And the way his dimples come out when he actually smiles. No, the man in front of me isn't a stranger.

It's Ashe.

The realization combined with one final nudge of my vibrator has me seeing stars as I tumble over the edge.

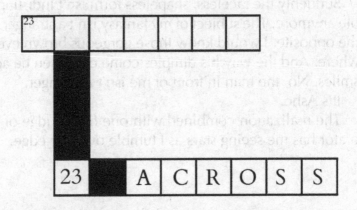

Another word for bravery.

November 15, 2024

Vic side-eyes me from across the lunchroom table.

I let out a long breath.

"I feel . . . weird about it," I admit.

It took me nearly a week to tell my friends about my awkward engagement with Stanley, but I haven't been able to get it . . . or *him* . . . out of my mind ever since. Journaling didn't help. So . . . here I am I guess. I'm not quite sure whether or not I want them to convince me I'm a sane person. Maybe this would be easier if I was dreaming everything up in my mind.

"I can honestly say I've never felt 'weird' about having an orgasm before," Jo says.

"Not about that part! About the . . . you know . . ."

Mira puts her fork back in her mason jar with a loud clink. "Fantasies are totally normal," she says. "I have them all the time."

I bite down hard, making my jaw flex. "This was . . . a first for me." I look up at my friends from above my glasses. "Usually they don't have a face."

Mira gives me a disgusted look.

"No, I mean, they don't have a specific face. Except this one did and . . . I kind of . . . liked it?"

The three of them say a loud and dramatic "aw" all at the same time.

I can't stop the heat that rushes to my cheeks.

"It's probably all nonsense anyway," I say dismissively. "I was tired and I had spent most of the day with him. He probably just popped into my mind at a weird time. That's all."

Vic sips at their coffee.

"Yes," they hum, "very unusual for you to think of him while you're about to . . . lift off."

I would love nothing more than to be swallowed up by the ground right now.

Is that too much to ask?

As usual, the universe doesn't respond.

"Any plans for the weekend?" Jo asks. I send them a mental thank you for changing the subject. They give me a slight nod in response.

"Snow's coming, so you know what that means," Vic says as they lean into their partner.

"Oh no, snowed in. Whatever shall we do?" Jo pretends to faint dramatically.

Vic tilts their head up and whispers something in Jo's ear. It takes less than a second for their face to turn red. I can only imagine what must have prompted that reaction. Then again, maybe I don't want to know.

"We're doing a *Twilight* marathon," Mira says excitedly. "I finally convinced Tony to watch them with me."

"True love," Jo and Vic say together.

"Soon, you'll be riding off into the sunset together while quoting *The Princess Bride*," I add.

Mira looks up at the roof with glazed eyes. "Ah, the dream."

Jo takes a long sip of their iced latte. "What about you, L?"

I finish working on my bite of sandwich and put the rest down before answering.

"It's my turn to check the cabin this weekend," I tell them. "So I'll probably just bunker in and wait out the storm."

"Sounds like a great time to catch up on some reading," Mira says. "Have you finished your book yet?"

I shake my head. "It's been too busy with work and trying to wrap my head around how to try these new assessment strategies. I'll bring it with me this weekend though. You're right. It's the perfect opportunity."

The five-minute warning bell rings, and we all tuck our lunches away.

I push open the door and hold it for my friends as they walk though.

"Drive safe!" Mira says as she leaves.

"Yeah, let us know when you get there!"

"I will!" I call from behind them as we go our separate ways.

"You sure you want to drive in the storm?"

I turn around to find Ashe standing on the other side of the open door. I let it swing closed.

Images of him on top of me while I squirm and writhe with pleasure flash behind my eyes.

Get a fucking grip.

"Yeah," I try to say, but it comes out hoarse, as if I'm choking on air.

I cough to clear my throat. "I'm off to the family cabin this weekend."

"Everything okay?" he asks as he puts his hands in his pockets and leans against the doorframe.

I nod. "It's just my turn to check on things. You know, to keep the insurance company happy."

He lets out a low chuckle. "Fair enough."

"You should really see it some time, it's gorgeous out there."

Ashe gives me a warm smile. "I'd like that."

Something in my gut tugs like a child wanting attention. It's impossible to ignore, and yet I'm still somewhat apprehensive about it. I swallow my nerves anyway. After all, if there is a storm coming, it would be foolish to go alone, right? Plus, we still haven't gone stargazing.

Is that a reason or an excuse to spend more time with him?

"Would you maybe want to come with me?" I ask. "We still haven't had a chance to watch the stars."

It feels impossible, but somehow I maintain eye contact with him.

"You don't think the storm will get in the way?"

He has a point.

I spare a glance at the weather app on my phone. "It says the snow isn't supposed to start until close to midnight. And since it's clear right now, we should be safe. Plus, the weather is so unpredictable this time of year. We could get three flakes or a foot of snow. No one knows. So I'll leave the decision up to you."

His grin widens. "I'm sure I can clear my schedule," he says.

"Don't go out of your way," I tease.

"For you? Never." The skin at Ashe's temples creases as he gives me a knowing smile.

Students make their way past us in a rush to get to their next classes.

"I have to go," I say. "Time to change lives and all that."

"I have no doubt."

I follow the students down the hall, grinning like Cupid's fool all the while.

It's hard to imagine that we have a snowstorm on the way. I have the windows rolled down Dad's old GMC, with one hand on the steering wheel and the other hanging out the window. The roads are too unpredictable for Charlie, my car, out here, so we always take Old Red. There's no temperature gauge in the truck, but when I checked the weather report before I left, it was still fifteen degrees outside. But I know Southern Alberta and how quickly her weather changes. She sure keeps the meteorologists on their toes.

My long hair flies around my head like Medusa's snakes from the wind through the open window. Ashe swats at it with his hand as a few tendrils weave their way over to attack him.

"Hey!" he exclaims.

I just laugh as he bats at my hair as if it's a persistent bug. Usually I have it tied back, but there's something so freeing about having the fresh air comb through it. I almost forgot how at home I feel on these country roads.

"Hold on tight," I tell him. "This is the easy part of the ride."

I take a right turn onto an old gravel road. It twists and turns through the hills, winding around them like a track of stretch marks over skin: a sign of a path well-traveled.

"Wow," Ashe says as we crest the hill. "It's like a whole new world out here."

He's right. The rolling hills bleed into the forest as we make our way farther west. With each passing minute, the brush gets thicker and thicker, until all that is left is a wall of trees on either side and the dusty gravel road.

"Beautiful, isn't it?"

He nods, eyes fixed on the sights outside his window.

I wonder what kind of magic he sees beyond the glass. I've made this drive so many times that some of the smaller details no longer jump out at me. I'm almost jealous that he gets to see this for the first time and experience everything this way. Almost. There's a different, but no less potent magic that comes with anticipating being in your favorite place in the world, seeing it in your mind's eye and breathing it in, even with your eyes closed. One day, Ashe will have that too.

I take another right turn onto a narrow dirt road.

"We're almost there," I tell him, "but this part might . . . well, let's just say you should definitely keep your arms in the vehicle at all times and keep your seatbelt on. It gets a little bumpy."

"It can't be that ba—"

Ashe is cut off as we hit the first pothole. Years ago, we were able to navigate around them, but now . . . not so much. They're everywhere.

Ashe's arm flies up to hold on to his "holy shit" handle and I have to hold back a laugh.

"I told you that you were in for a ride. Better saddle up, cowboy, we're just getting started."

Ten minutes and several rounds of colorful language later, we pull into the dirt driveway to the A-frame cabin.

Ashe lets out a long breath. "It's a good thing I don't get car sick," he says.

"I don't know, you look pretty green to me," I tease.

He gives me a disapproving glare.

"It's the forrestents," he says with a wink before getting out of the truck.

I roll my eyes at the poorly executed *Twilight* joke and follow him out.

"Well"—I put my bag down and unlock the door—"welcome to the best place on Earth."

The familiar smell of firewood and pine needles wafts toward me as I open the door. My shoulders and jaw relax, and I take in a long, deep breath. The inside is small, just a combined living room and kitchen with a spiral staircase that leads up to the loft. But despite its size, it always feels as if it holds the wonders of the world inside it to me. Like if I look hard enough while I'm here, I'll find all the answers to the unasked questions of the universe.

"You can take the loft if you want," I tell him as I gesture to the stairs. "I've slept on this couch enough that it's basically molded to my frame." I run my hand along the lines of the old burgundy upholstery.

"I don't mind staying here if you'd rather have the bed," he says. "I've never slept in front of a fireplace before. Maybe I can tick it off my list."

I shrug. "Suit yourself. But just so you know, if you sleep in front of the fire, you're responsible for keeping it going throughout the night."

"Fine by me."

Ashe puts his bag down on the floor beside the couch before turning to take a look around.

"So, that's the kitchen, obviously," I say as I point toward the corner fitted with a two-burner stove and microwave. "And you've already seen the living room." I take a few steps toward the staircase. "The loft is up there. It's just a bed and some old bookshelves—nothing fancy. And if you need the bathroom, it's just around the corner here."

I lead Ashe around the staircase to the small room behind the kitchen. There's a toilet, a sink, and a standing shower in the corner which I barely fit in.

"We can't drink the water from the tap, so make sure you fill from the water jugs by the front door."

Ashe nods and stands to the side to let me out of the cramped space.

"I know it's not much," I say, "but it's cozy, and in a lot of ways, it's home."

"It's perfect," he breathes. "I can see why you love it so much."

I give him a warm smile.

There's something special about sharing this space with him. Just like when he met Pops for the first time. Seeing him here, sitting on the couch laughing with me, it's as if he was meant to be here all along, and I can't help but think that maybe we were meant to be here together too.

ARTWORK DRAWN BY
honeyy pears
honeyypears♡

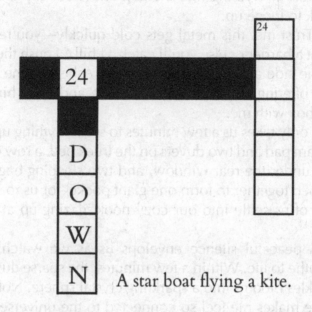

24 DOWN

A star boat flying a kite.

November 15, 2024

The first rule of stargazing in the back of a pickup truck on an old gravel road is always bring blankets. And snacks. Preferably both.

"Is that it?" Ashe asks as I dump an armful of blankets into the truck box.

"Not even close," I say as I turn to grab another load.

Ashe follows me back into the cabin and takes the foam pad in one arm and the bag of goodies in his other. Our steps are accompanied by the soft readjustment of the rocks beneath our feet as we make our way toward the tailgate. He lifts the latch with ease and slowly lets the heavy metal plate down.

"What's all this for?"

I toss everything into the box and brace my arms on the truck to lunge up.

"Trust me, this metal gets cold quickly—you're going to want a barrier or else you'll catch a chill." I push the blankets to the side and take the foam from Ashe. "Come on up," I say, offering him a hand. He takes it, and I pull him up into the box with me.

It only takes us a few minutes to set everything up. There's a foam pad and two duvets on the truck bed, a row of pillows just under the rear window, and two sleeping bags that we zipped together to form one giant pocket for us to sit in. The two of us settle into our cozy nook, gazing up at the night sky.

A peaceful silence envelops us as we watch the stars breathe to life. Within a few minutes, the sparse dust of silver freckles blooms into a sparkling crystal sphere. Nothing ever quite makes me feel so connected to the universe as if witnessing the stars wake up for the night.

Ashe sucks in a breath beside me.

"Was it worth the wait?" I ask him.

He relaxes back, bracing an arm behind his head, never breaking his gaze from the lights above us.

"Definitely," he says.

"You really never saw the stars before?"

Ashe lets out a low hum.

"Not like this. Sometimes, if Nan and I were driving back from something at night, we would take the long way home, and catch a few dots in the sky from the car. It wasn't something I ever thought about much. There was always something on the news from NASA or a new photo in *National Geographic* that made me feel as if I experienced it secondhand. But this"—he trails his fingers through the air in front of him—"is so much more than what a picture could paint."

I can't imagine living three decades without ever meeting the stars face-to-face. My childhood was filled with late nights by a campfire, watching the orange sparks transform into silver dots in the night sky. They're as familiar as my friends are to me. Sometimes it feels as if I know their patterns better than I know myself.

When I finally find my favorite constellation, I point up to draw Ashe's attention to it. "You see this little cluster of stars here that kind of looks like a boat? And then there's a little line with a diamond shape at the end?"

Ashe moves closer to me so he can look down my arm to find the place in the sky. I can feel his warmth through his shirt, and there's a slight hint of mint on his breath from the peppermint schnapps in his hot chocolate.

"A boat flying a kite?"

I nod and slowly outline the constellation above us. "It's called Cetus. It's supposed to be a whale, I think."

Ashe shifts beside me. "That does not look like a whale."

I shrug. "I don't make the rules of star connections, but I'm happy to bend them to fit my definition if I need to."

Ashe laughs and lies back down on his side, letting a cool draft in between us.

"A true pioneer of the sciences," he remarks.

"I do what I can."

We spend the next several minutes looking up and discussing different silver-outlined shapes in the night sky. Ashe finds one that looks like an ocean wave.

"Is that a thing?"

I raise my hands up slightly. "No idea," I admit. "And I left my book of constellations at home, so we can't check. But, I guess if you want it to be a thing, then it's a thing."

Ashe nods. "The Thing constellation it is then."

The pure laughter that escapes from his chest is almost as sweet as the hot chocolate on my lips. When I turn my head,

I see Ashe looking back at me, his dark eyes sparkling in the soft starlight. My breath catches in my throat and a heat rises through my chest. I'm suddenly very thankful for the darkness, and I send up a silent prayer to the stars watching that it's enough to cover the blush surely blooming across my cheeks.

"Thank you for this, L," Ashe says as he reaches over and tucks a loose hair behind my ear. My skin burns from where his fingers brush against my cheekbone.

A fallen star dances in the air between us. No, not a star, the first snowflake of the night. When I look back up, the silver sparks begin to fade, dulled by the breath of clouds growing above us.

"I guess that's our sign to head back in," I say, still somewhat flustered and frustrated at the universe for not giving us another five minutes of bliss.

A small smile tugs at the edge of Ashe's lips as he pushes himself up. He extends a hand down to me, and I take it. The soft warmth of his palm seems to course up my arm in a flurry, causing me to suck in a sharp breath.

"Don't be so sad," he says, clearly recognizing the change in my tone and body language. "It's just time for the second act. It's the snow's turn to shine."

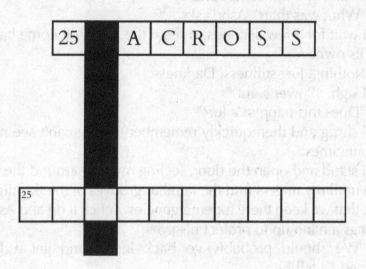

25 | A | C | R | O | S | S

25 | | | | | | | | |

An unexpected emotion.

November 15, 2024

The snowflakes seem to glitter against the dark night from the dim porch light. Ashe and I sit outside in the plastic lawn chairs, watching them fall like icy tears from the stars above. The hot chocolate warms our hands and bellies as we sit in the peaceful quiet of the brisk autumn night. Our breath dances with the falling stars in twirls of smoke up into the night sky.

Ashe leans back in his chair, eyes closed as if on a sunny beach, taking in every drop of sunlight instead of the dim flickering porchlight which we decided to turn back on so we wouldn't trip over the uneven deck boards.

"Taking in the sun—"

I'm interrupted as the lights on the porch blink out, casting a blanket of darkness around us.

"What was that?" Ashe asks.

I wait for a few seconds to see if the light will come back on its own.

Nothing. Just stillness. Darkness.

I sigh. "Power's out."

"Does this happen a lot?"

I shrug and then quickly remember that he can't see me. "Sometimes."

I stand and open the door, feeling my way around the table until my fingers find the familiar grooves of the flashlight hilt that we keep there for emergencies. I click it on and Ashe brings a hand up to protect his eyes.

"We should probably go back inside and get a fire started," I tell him.

I arrange the kindling on the bottom with a few pieces of scrap newspaper on top before lighting a match and tossing it in. Within a few seconds, we have a decent flame, so I add a small piece of wood to the side, careful not to snuff it out.

"You're good at this," Ashe remarks.

I raise a shoulder. "Years of practice," I tell him. "Pops had me try to light it without matches once."

"And how did that go?"

I brush my fingers through my hair and think back to the seemingly endless hours of twisting twigs and rocks.

"Some stories are best left in the past where they belong."

Ashe laughs. "Well, you can't be brilliant at everything," he says.

I frown at him and put my hands on my hips.

"I can certainly try," I say defiantly.

Ashe rolls his eyes and sits on the ground in front of the fire with a blanket wrapped around his one side. He holds the other side open for me.

"We'll probably stay warmer this way," he says.

I try to swallow down the sudden dryness in my throat. My heart jumps in my chest at the thought of snuggling next to him, the only light from the low embers and dancing flames.

"I don't bite."

I pinch my lips together. "That isn't necessarily reassuring," I say as I sit beside him.

Ashe's arm drapes over my shoulder and I pull the blanket around to cover my legs. And then, because I'm always bravest in the dark, I inch myself closer until I'm completely nestled against Ashe's warm body.

"Am I making you uncomfortable?" he asks.

I shake my head. "No," I say honestly. "This is actually . . . nice."

Ashe lets out a soft breath and relaxes around me. "I'm glad," he says. "To be here. Especially with you . . . I—"

I turn my head to look up at him. The flames reflect in his dark eyes, breathing another layer of warm life into them. His lashes cast long shadows over his cheeks like wings.

"Ashe?"

His throat works and his jaw flexes.

"Are you—"

"Ireallylikespendingtimewithyou," he blurts out.

He blinks and wipes the side of his eye with the back of his hand.

"I really like spending time with you," he says again, this time much slower.

My heart pounds to the rhythm of his words. I don't know if it's because of the fire or something else, but my whole body feels as if it's alive with heat.

"Me too."

I cast my eyes down and poke the tips of my fingers with my thumbnail.

There's a shuffling before I feel Ashe's warm hands on my chin, coaxing me back up.

I let him.

The second our eyes meet, it feels as if my chest cracks open. My heart is on the floor. No, it's bleeding in my hands and the only thing that could possibly put it back is his lips on mine.

"Ashe," I whisper.

He places a gentle kiss on my forehead. "Thank you for bringing joy back into my life, L," he says.

I can't breathe.

I can't move.

All I can feel is him. Every inch where we're touching, and every place we're not.

My thoughts are a tangled mess in my head. There are a thousand voices screaming at me to do something. Say something.

SAY SOMETHING!

"Have you ever been in love?"

Where the fuck did that come from?

Ashe tenses beside me, and I'm suddenly aware that my question may have come across the wrong way.

"Sorry, I don't know why I said that. I didn't mean—please ignore me. Please . . ."

Is it too late to run away forever? Change my name? Live off the land?

I hunch down in the blanket. Maybe it will swallow me up.

After a few moments, he relaxes and shakes his head. "I thought I was . . . once. But . . ."

I wait for him to continue, but after a minute passes, I'm convinced he won't on his own.

Ashe takes an arm out of our blanket to run a hand through his hair. The ends tickle the tips of his long eyelashes. The sudden gap lets in a breath of cold air and I shiver.

"I . . ." he starts again. "I thought I was, but things ended and I . . . didn't care? I was just relieved. It felt like . . . saving myself. The only thing I was torn up about was telling my friends and my parents. They really liked her. They all thought I was going to marry her. Hell, I thought I would marry her one day too. It's just how it works, right? At least, that's what I thought. That's what I expected, what I thought everyone expected. But I think it was the idea of her that I loved, not her. It's not fair, I know . . ."

Ashe lets out a long sigh, and his shoulders slump forward, making him seem small and frail.

"I hope you don't think less of me for it," he says softly. A whisper nearly lost among the crackling wood.

Instinctively, I reach over and take his other hand under the blanket. I don't know what to say. I've never been engaged, or nearly engaged. My friends and family have never given me any kind of pressure to get married. I've had partners, but none of them had been serious. It just never felt right. But this? I could never imagine being in his position. Whether the pressure was intentional or not, the effect was the same.

"It's not fair," I say before completely thinking it through.

Ashe stiffens beside me again.

I shake my head.

"Sorry, that's not what I meant. I meant that it's not fair to you. You deserve to have a life filled with love which overflows from every person in it. Not expectations and settled relations. You deserve more than that."

He brings his head up and his tear-glazed eyes meet mine. "You really believe that, don't you?" he asks.

I nod. "Of course I do."

Ashe's eyes move down my face and settle on my lips. A shiver rushes up though me despite the heat from the fire and the blanket around us. There's a flush that I can feel spreading up from my chest. He pulls his lip ring into his mouth with his teeth as he studies me. He swallows as he brings his gaze back up to mine.

"Is that . . . something *you* want?" I somehow manage to ask him.

A gentle smile tugs across his face as he reaches his hand out to cup my cheek.

"I never thought I would be so lucky to meet someone who would ever care enough to ask me that question."

I let myself lean into his touch, heart pounding in my ears, and pray that it's not loud enough that he can hear it too.

"Is that . . . a yes?" I ask.

My gaze trails down to his lips as well, and I wonder, not for the first time, what it would be like to pull that ring into my mouth.

"Fuck yes."

Ashe's grip tightens in my hair as he crashes our lips together, setting every nerve under my skin on fire.

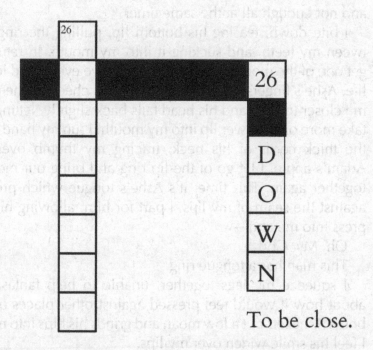

26 DOWN

To be close.

November 15, 2024

The heat in my chest explodes all over my body in a torrent and settles deep in my belly. Ashe's lips, which started out soft and gentle, now move with a desperate intensity. His hands wander down my neck and back before they settle just under my hips. He drags me up onto his lap, the blanket falling from around us into a heap on the floor.

He's not the only one who can't keep his hands to himself. Before I even realize it, my fingers are laced in his hair, pulling him in closer to me as if I'm starved for breath, and he is the only air left in the world. Ashe groans as he pushes his hips up against me. Even through his jeans I can feel his hardening length pushing against the soft fabric of my leggings.

Another wave of fire courses through my veins. It's too much and not enough all at the same time.

I bite down, teasing his bottom lip, pulling the ring between my teeth, and sucking it into my mouth. In return, I get one of the most satisfying sounds I have ever heard in my life. Ashe's fingers press deep into my ass cheeks as he pulls me closer to him, and his head falls back slightly, letting me take more of his lower lip into my mouth. I run my hand over the thick cords of his neck, tracing my thumb over his Adam's apple. I let go of the lip ring and bring our mouths together again. This time, it's Ashe's tongue which presses against the seam of my lips. I part for him, allowing him to press into me and—

Oh. My. God.

This man has a tongue ring.

I squeeze my legs together, unable to help fantasizing about how it would feel pressed against other places of my body. Ashe lets out a low moan and grinds his hips into mine. I feel his smile widen over my lips.

"Surprise." The word comes out as more of a low hum than anything else and I have to suppress a whimper.

Impulsively, I grab at the neck of his shirt. My brain has completely left my body. I'm operating on pure instinct and desire now. And that instinct is telling me that there are far too many articles of clothing between us.

Ashe breaks our kiss and leans back. His fingers tug at the bottom hem of his shirt, and I can almost see the thoughts going through his head.

Shit. I took it too far. I wasn't even thinking.

"I'm sorry," I say, sitting up. "I shouldn't have—"

Ashe raises his hand up and traces my bottom lip with his thumb, silencing me. "It's okay," he whispers. "I want to."

He slowly reaches behind himself and pulls his shirt up, over his head, revealing a long tattoo of a bird which traces the side of his body. The wings stretch up and over each shoulder, and it's posed in such a way that it looks as if it's protecting him. As I examine the intricate lines, I realize that it's not just a bird. I've seen something like it before.

"A phoenix?" I ask.

Ashe nods.

"Rising from the ashes," I mumble under my breath.

"I know it's probably a bit corny, but—"

"I love it."

There are several stretch marks that extend up his stomach, and I pass over them gently, embracing every part of him.

"You know," I say, "these could be the flames."

Ashe looks into my eyes, the light from the fire dancing in his almost golden irises. He looks so soft. So genuine. So pure. And I swear something in my chest cracks in the way that his gaze pierces mine.

Slowly, I pull my shirt up over my head and toss it to the side. My long hair falls down my back, tickling my newly exposed skin. Ashe's eyes trace down my body until they land on my black sports bra.

He reaches up to the zipper at the front and brings his gaze back to mine.

"May I?" he asks.

I nod.

In a smooth, gentle motion, Ashe unzips my bra, leaving my heavy breasts free in front of me. I bite my lip as I flick the fabric onto my shirt pile. Then I run my fingertips over the lines of black ink at his side, making Ashe twitch under my touch.

A wry smile spreads across my face.

"Someone's ticklish," I tease as I go over the same spot again.

185

Ashe's gaze darkens as he wraps his arms around me. In an instant, we switch places. I let out a high-pitched squeak as he takes my hands in his and pins them above my head. Slowly, nearly agonizingly so, he places a row of kisses down from my ear, over my neck until he settles on my collarbone. I feel the hairs on my arms and neck rise as he runs his teeth over my sensitive skin.

"Is this okay?" he asks me.

I'm so far gone that I barely register the words.

Ashe stops his kisses and looks down at me with heavy-lidded eyes.

"Don't stop," I say breathlessly. "Please don't stop."

His shoulders relax and he places another kiss on my lips, this one soft and full of promise. He moves to nuzzle his head into my neck.

"What do you want?" The warmth from his breath sends a shock through to my core.

"What?" My thoughts are a scrambled mess.

His teeth are back on my neck, and he follows with another row of kisses.

"What do you like, L? What do you want?"

My mind flashes back to his tongue ring, and suddenly I can't get the image of him between my legs out of my head. I squeeze my thighs together again at the thought.

"Mmmm," he hums against me, pressing himself into my hips. "Fuck, L. Tell me what just went through your mind."

"You," I answer.

Ashe groans into my neck again. "What about me?"

I swallow, trying to form the words from the images in my head before translating them into English. Then I flush at the thought of actually voicing my desires.

"No, L. Don't do this to me," he pleads. "Don't trap yourself. Tell me. What. Do. You. Want?"

There's an urgency to his tone, and a desperation behind each word as he carefully annunciates them.

He releases my hands and wraps an arm behind my back, pulling me up into him. I arch with the movement, and my head falls back, leaving my throat completely exposed. He blows gently against it, and something bright and hot flashes through me.

"You!" I cry out. "Your tongue . . . on me . . . in me," I say between deep, panting breaths.

Ashe's satisfied groan vibrates over my skin.

"Tell me where."

I can't. I'm all out of words. So instead, I spread my legs and push his head down with my free hand. He doesn't resist. Something tells me that he was expecting this all along— he just wanted me to admit it myself.

There. Right there.

Ashe places a kiss where my legs meet, and the sensation sends me squirming beneath him. He pushes my body up slightly and nips at the top of my leggings. The sight of him with my pants in his mouth and his large dark eyes fixed on mine isn't something that will leave my mind any time soon.

He lets go of the fabric and it snaps against my stomach, leaving a warm sting behind.

"Off?" he asks, raising an eyebrow.

"Yes," I breathe.

Ashe's thumbs hook under the waistband and he pulls down until my pants gather at my ankles. Almost reverently, he gently tugs them the rest of the way off, massaging the back of my calves along the way. After tossing my leggings onto the couch behind us, he moves back up my body and places his first two fingers on top of the fabric of my black thong. Slowly, he trails lower and lower to the place where the fabric parts my ass. Then he moves back up to the spot where I'm sure I've soaked through by now.

Embarrassed, I tuck my head down and avoid his gaze.

"Eyes on me." Ashe's voice is low and smooth, enveloping us both in its richness. "I don't want you to miss anything."

Fuck.

My toes curl and I part my legs further for him.

Ashe smiles as he pushes my panties to the side and slips a finger through my wetness. He hums in approval and licks me off of him. His tongue ring glides up to the top before flicking back into his mouth. And not once does his gaze leave mine.

A low moan escapes me. I can't help it. I'm desperate. And this is torture.

Ashe slides his fingers under the waist of my thong.

In one quick motion, I'm bared to him. Heat from his gaze, the fire, and this insatiable desire coursing through me settles between my legs. I instinctively bring my knees together, but Ashe places a palm on my inner thigh and strokes upwards.

"Relax, L." He kisses my sensitive skin just above my knee. "You're safe." Another kiss. This time higher. "You are so fucking sexy." Higher again. One more kiss, and he'd be there. "Do you want this?" he asks, his head hovering just above where I need him most.

I nod, biting my lip, trying not to look too desperate.

"Use your words."

I let go of a long breath and lose myself in his dark gaze. A stray hair plays in his eyelashes and I brush it away.

"Yes . . . fuck yes."

The contact nearly sends me into oblivion on the spot.

This is way better than I could have ever dreamed—

Oh god, is that—

Ashe flattens his tongue and runs it up through the seam of my labia, and the nearly invisible ball that I haven't been able to stop thinking about stops right where I need it to.

"Fuck!"

I arch my back and Ashe's hands wrap around under me to grip my ass. He pulls me in closer to his mouth and slowly moves his tongue up and down. Every flick sends me higher and higher. I don't know when it happened, but both of my hands are in his hair, holding his face into me. When he dips into my opening, I nearly cry out again. He pushes up, sending a searing pleasure through my nerves.

Ashe pulls away slightly, and he removes his right arm from my back. With an eerie, seductive grace, he sucks a finger into his mouth, then two.

"I want to feel you pulse around me as you come undone," he says as he moves his hand back to my core. The tips of his fingers gently push at my entrance and I find myself grinding against him. Ashe lets out a low breath. "Do you want that too?"

My hands grip his hair even tighter and he groans in response.

"Yes," I whisper.

He's gentle at first, although I wish he wasn't, slowly entering me, watching me, checking to make sure everything feels good. Finally, when I've stretched for him, he begins to curl his fingers inside me. I immediately buck my hips up because fuck . . . that spot has never felt so fucking good in my life.

"Easy, L." Ashe's voice is low and husk. "We're just getting started."

Slowly, almost deliberately and methodically, he strokes my inner wall while he works my clit with his tongue. There's a gentle and patient grace to his every move. He makes me feel like some kind of divine being worthy of worship. As if there is nothing more important in this world right now than being here with me, exploring my body and giving me a pleasure fit for royalty.

I reflexively tense as he dips his tongue into me again, this time with his fingers still pushing on my inner wall. I'm granted a low moan in response as he caresses the side of my body with his other hand. My fingers clench in his hair and I arch back, letting him sink deeper into me.

"That's it," he purrs. The vibrations from his voice are nearly enough to send me over the edge.

Ashe's fingers push up as he takes a long, almost agonizing lick up to my clit. This time, he's less gentle. The sound of his fingers stroking in and out of me is perhaps the most erotic thing I've ever heard. Ashe sucks and keeps the pressure as he makes small, consistent licks against me. With every tap of his tongue ring, my pleasure grows. It rises higher and higher and threatens to drown me. I can't breathe. I can't think. And suddenly I'm there. I'm here. But I'm also not. I'm everywhere and nowhere all at once. I squeeze my eyes shut and let wave after wave crash through my body.

Someone's screaming. Maybe it's me, or maybe my soul has just been completely stripped from my being and slammed back into my body. I can't feel my fingers. All I see are tiny spots of light flickering around. I think I'm floating— suspended in time and space. And it's just us. There is only Ashe's warm breath against my stomach, and his light feather touches across my collarbone and around my breasts. He's whispering something into me, but I can't hear him. I only sense the rumble from his chest and the low vibrations of his voice.

He holds me tight as I come down from the most extreme orgasm I have ever had in my life. I nuzzle into his bare chest, just over the head of the phoenix. I can feel more than hear his heart beating through his flushed skin.

Ba-dum ba-dum. Ba-dum ba-dum.

Is it possible to crawl into someone's chest? Something tells me that I could comfortably live in Ashe's heart forever. Maybe that's a blessing reserved for higher beings.

"Are you okay?" he asks, stroking a hair from my face.

I nod and tilt my head up to kiss him.

Ashe's thumb traces my cheekbone as he pulls me up to his lips. My senses spark back to life at the contact. Carefully, I pull myself up to straddle him.

How the hell does he still have these jeans on?

I trail my hands down his soft belly and undo the button of his pants. His cock strains against the zipper, and by the time I have it down, his erection pushes proudly up against his boxer briefs.

Ashe lets out a low sigh of what could only be relief as he lifts his hips and allows me to pull his pants all the way off.

Now, what to do about the rest?

I lean over him and run my teeth along the waistband. I wonder for a moment if I would be able to take his underwear off with just my mouth. But just as I am contemplating the mechanics of such a maneuver, Ashe takes my chin with his hand and forces me up to look at him. His heavy-lidded eyes are dark and full of lust.

"L," he groans, almost as if he's in pain. Have I hurt him?

Ashe pauses before saying anything else, as if weighing his thoughts. His next words come out in a flurry.

"I'm a patient man, but if you don't take these off in the next thirty seconds, I'm going to blow my load in my pants without ever feeling those delicious lips around my cock, and that would feel like more of a sin than anything I've ever done in my life."

Warmth floods my core and I have to force my legs together to relieve some of the pressure growing between them.

In a single, swift motion, I pull his underwear down past his knees. They fall in a heap by his feet, leaving him completely exposed.

Without a doubt, I am in the presence of the most beautiful human being ever to grace this earth. Ashe is perfection. I can't imagine a single part of him being any different. His eyes sparkle in the light of the fire, and I let out a low gasp.

"You're beautiful." The words come out of my mouth just as fast as I think them. Then embarrassment flushes my cheeks and I look down at my knees.

Beautiful? Really?

"Sorry, do you prefer handsome? I mean, you're definitely handsome too, it's just you're so beautiful—"

"L," Ashe says softly, interrupting me by running his thumb over my lower lip. "To be called beautiful by you is a blessing."

I wet my lips with my tongue and graze the tip of his finger on the way. I'm rewarded with a twitch of his dick. I look down and find a satisfying bead of precum dripping down from the tip. I can't help myself—I have to know what he tastes like.

I trail my fingers up the insides of his legs. Just as I'm about to reach the top of his inner thigh, Ashe lets out a low moan. His head falls back slightly and his breath catches.

Someone has a sweet spot.

Slowly, I run my thumb along the same spot, testing to see what kind of reaction I can get from him.

"Fuck . . ."

Something about that word and the way it rolls off Ashe's tongue makes my brain calm. The torrent that usually occupies every corner of my mind now feels like a still lake. I can breathe here. And it feels so good.

I trace the vein that runs along his length all the way up to the seam.

Out of nowhere, Ashe grabs my wrist and sits up. His chest and cheeks are flushed, and he takes several panting breaths before he speaks.

"Careful."

I swallow hard. The intensity of his stare threatens to pierce through me.

"Careful . . . good?"

He gives a nearly imperceptible nod of his head.

"Careful really fucking good," he agrees. "Right here." He moves my thumb over the ridge right under the head of his cock. "That's . . . shit." Ashe takes a few more breaths, still carefully moving my hand around his length. His eyes squeeze shut, and it almost looks as if he's in pain.

"Is this okay?" I ask him.

"This is . . . perfect . . . Just be gentle." Ashe relaxes and lets go of my hand before leaning back again. "Be gentle with me."

Be gentle with me.

His words, more of a prayer, swim through the air between us, enveloping us in a spell that we could have never expected to cast only a few months ago.

Something pangs in my chest. It's lighter than air and heavier than steel all at the same time. It makes me want to cry out in ecstasy and throw up. A part of me feels terrified, as if I'm falling at top speed. Another side of me is overwhelmed from the thrill.

This isn't just joy. This is . . . something . . . more. I have never been more scared. And I have never felt more alive.

"Always," I say as I finally lower my head and part my lips around the tip of his cock

Ashe tenses underneath me and reaches up to wrap his fingers in my hair, pulling it out of my face. Then, almost hesitantly, he guides me down, farther and farther until he reaches the back of my throat. As I come back up, I let my tongue rest on the sensitive spot I found earlier, making small flicks up and down.

Almost immediately, Ashe's grip tightens, and a spark of hot pain radiates through my scalp. It's quickly replaced by a rush of pleasure and a sense of pride. This is all me. All of Ashe's reactions are because he's enjoying this. Maybe even as much as I am.

I bob up and down on his cock, circling the base with one hand as I focus on the head with my mouth. Ashe doesn't press me to go deeper. If anything, his fingers through my hair are just another point of connection. He doesn't do any more than guide me over his length, all the while making delicious sounds of pleasure that I wish I could wrap up and save forever. When I hollow my cheeks, sucking him down as much as I dare, Ashe pulses hard in my mouth, and he pushes his hips up to meet me.

"Sorry," he breathes. "Reflex."

I come back up, placing a gentle kiss right on the tip.

"Don't be sorry," I tell him, circling the head with my tongue. "I liked it."

Ashe meets my gaze. His eyes are little more than dark pools of lust, and fuck if that doesn't turn me on even more.

"L." My name from his lips comes out more like a growl.

"Yes," I say, licking that sensitive spot again.

His eyes roll back slightly, his eyelashes fluttering over his cheeks like butterfly kisses.

"My pants . . . back pocket . . . wallet . . . condom."

I almost laugh from the way his words come out. He is picture-perfect. I love seeing how vulnerable he is under-neath me. And all mine. At least for the night.

And maybe longer . . . if you let him.

I rummage through his splayed pants and open the brown faux leather wallet. My eyes catch on the corner of some kind of silver foil.

Bingo.

"I have an IUD," I tell him. "Just . . . so you know."

"Okay," he says, a little breathless. "I still insist."

This time, I do let out a little giggle.

"It wasn't a condom rejection, Ashe. It was just to help put you more at ease."

He does relax a bit at that.

"Good."

I rip the package and pinch the tip of the condom over him.

"Do you want to do the honors?" I ask.

Ashe shakes his head.

"By all means."

I slowly roll the latex down his length until it lands snug against the base. It's interesting though—there's some kind of residue on top that's on my fingers now.

"Is that . . . lube?"

Ashe smirks and raises himself to rest on his elbows behind him.

"If I said yes, would that be a bad thing?"

"No," I say, more intrigued than anything. "Not at all. It's just . . . different."

"I like different."

"Me too."

The heat from the fire at my back does nothing to stop the shiver that runs over my skin. Then I realize my fingers are starting to tingle. Like the chill in my mouth after chewing minty gum. Water always feels a thousand times colder after that.

"It's cooling," Ashe says, following my gaze to my fingertips. "Have you tried that before?"

I shake my head.

"It's also . . . sensation heightening. Or at least that's what the package says. I wouldn't know. No vagina and all."

I laugh again. "Really?"

I crawl on top of him, straddling his hips. I press his cock between us and grind up against his length.

He shrugs, but a playful smile tugs at the edge of his lips. I lean myself over and kiss them, taking that blissful ring into my mouth once again.

Ashe removes his arms from behind him and we fall to the ground together. His hands caress the dips and curves of my body as he explores every inch of my skin. It's only been a few seconds, but I can already feel my clit tingling, and he was right. It is sensation-enhancing because fuck . . . I could come just from this. But I'm greedy. I want more.

I reluctantly pull away from his mouth and position the tip of his cock at my entrance.

"Are you ready?" I ask him.

"Fuck yes," he says almost instantaneously. "Are you?"

In answer, I sink down onto him, letting him stretch me so slowly that it's almost deliciously torturous. Inch by inch, I slide down until he's fully seated inside me. Then, with one fluid motion, I grind forward.

The feeling is unlike any kind of pleasure I have felt before. The spot that he reaches inside me seems to send a lightning bolt straight to my brain, until all I can see is sparks of white. So I do it again. And again. And again. Until tears start to sting at my eyes.

I've never cried from sex before, but there's a first for everything.

"Fuck, L," Ashe grunts as he palms my ass.

"I—"

My words are cut off as Ashe thrusts himself up while holding my hips down.

I let out a soft whimper and throw my head back.

"Yes," Ashe whispers, "just like that. Fuck, you feel so good."

I thought I was hot before, but that was nothing compared to the blazing inferno which now scorches every inch of my body.

Ash sits up, and I wrap my legs around his waist. He nuzzles his face between my breasts and sucks in a sharp breath.

"I could stay here forever and die the happiest man on Earth," he murmurs into my skin. "If you'd have me."

"Of course I'll have you, Ashe." I moan as my back bows. "Always."

I fall apart in his arms and he catches me as I fall down, down, down, until my vision goes black and all I can hear is the heavy thumping of his heart underneath his scorching hot skin.

Gently, he rolls us over until he's on top of me and I am lying on the soft carpet looking up into his beautiful dark round eyes. I reach up and stroke a stray hair away from his face. Ashe places a warm, gentle kiss on my forehead before moving down and claiming my mouth with his. I part my lips and allow his tongue to explore. Just when I feel the heavy warmth starting to grow in my stomach again, he pulses inside me.

I suck in a sharp breath.

"Ready for another round?" he asks, teasing me with slow, reverent strokes.

"Yes," I moan, not wanting to wait another moment to experience the same blissful euphoria as before.

Ashe slowly moves in and out of me, setting every nerve on fire. My fingernails rake through the skin on his back as I cry out his name.

"More!"

"Are you sure?" he asks.

"Yes"—I gasp. "Please," I beg.

Ashes pace quickens, and I feel my blood racing through my veins so hot, so fast, drumming through my ears, deafening me. I'm almost there . . . I can feel it . . . so close I can almost taste it . . . can see it . . . if I reach out just a little closer—

"That's it . . . right . . . there," Ashe groans as he thrusts his hips up so that he hits that special place inside of me.

Fuck.

"Oh shit, I'm going to—"

Ashe lets out a low moan and I come completely undone in his arms again.

Ashe shakes, and I feel him pulse inside of me as his whole body goes hard and rigid through his climax. He lowers himself gently on top of me, laying a trail of kisses down from my ear all the way to my collarbone.

"You're like a dream," he says. "This can't be real."

I lace my fingers in his hair, pulling him closer. I run my hand up and down his back as our heavy breathing slowly begins to even out.

"It's real, Ashe," I say, "and I still never want to wake up."

After a few minutes, Ashe slowly gets up and disposes of the condom in the kitchen garbage. He comes back with a damp cloth, and after warming it up in front of the fire, he carefully wipes down my body from head to toe, paying special, gentle attention to me while cleaning between my legs. I've never been cared for so thoroughly, and it sends another burst of warmth through my chest. He places the cloth on the ground beside him and wraps the blanket around both of us before reaching down to lace his fingers with mine. I grip Ashe's hand tightly and lean my head against his shoulder. The heat from the fire wraps us in a warm embrace. I know this moment won't last forever, but for a second, I pretend it will and let it completely sink under my skin and settle deep into my bones.

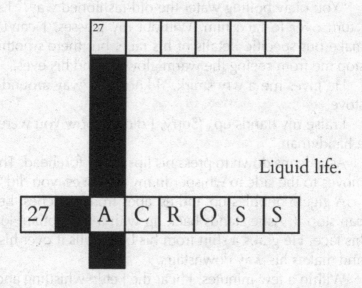

Liquid life.

| 27 | A | C | R | O | S | S |

November 16, 2024

As it turned out, no one needed to sleep on the couch after all.

Ashe rolls over onto his side, pulling me into his chest. I curl into his embrace and interlace my fingers in his, holding his hand over my heart.

"Good morning," he whispers into my ear before kissing my neck.

I can't help the shiver that runs up my spine.

"Good morning," I say, squeezing his hand tighter against me.

The faint rays from the sunrise peek through the curtains, casting a warm glow onto me. I could stay here forever, wrapped in Ashe's embrace, breathing in the fresh scent of pine, basking in the morning sun.

"Coffee?" Ashe asks before placing a kiss on my cheek and rolling out of bed.

"You okay boiling water the old-fashioned way?" I ask as I turn over to face him. Without my glasses, I can't quite make out specific details of his face, but there's nothing to stop me from seeing the warm glow behind his eyes.

He gives me a wry smirk. "I know my way around a gas stove."

I raise my hands up. "Sorry, I didn't know you were such a handyman."

Ashe leans down to press his lips to my forehead. Then he moves to the side to whisper in my ear. "Yes, you did."

A giggle bubbles up and escapes from my chest before I can stop it. Ashe stands back up with a triumphant look on his face. He grabs a shirt from his bag, pulls it over his head and makes his way downstairs.

Within a few minutes, I hear the kettle whistling and a jar opening.

I'm down in my hoodie and shorts just as Ashe is pouring.

The warm mug feels delightful in my frosty hands, and although the liquid burns a bit going down, I'm thankful for it.

"We should probably head back into town and call someone to come check it out," I tell him.

The storm wasn't nearly as bad as the weatherman predicted, but without any service out here, no one will know that the power is off. Flipping the breakers didn't do anything, so it's out of my hands.

Ashe nods as he sips at his coffee. "Is it bad of me to say that I could gladly stay here, tucked away from the world, indefinitely?"

I shake my head. "Not at all. This place has that effect on people. Why do you think I come up here every chance I get?"

He smirks. "Now you're just making me jealous on purpose."

I tilt my head to the side. "Your words not mine."

We tidy up the few dishes and put everything back before cleaning out the fireplace and assembling a new stack of kindling for the next person who comes up. It's never a long enough stay at the cabin, but just one night feels as if I'm forced to boomerang back to reality. A part of me wants to kick and scream like a toddler and yell at the universe for being unfair, but if I've learned anything over the years, it's that the universe couldn't give two shits about fairness.

We keep the windows up on the drive back. Fortunately, the snow has sunk into a few of the potholes on the dirt path, so it's not as bumpy on the way out to the gravel road. Ashe doesn't even reach up to hold on for his dear life, which is almost a shame. I admit, it's fun keeping him on his toes.

"You mind if I turn on the radio? It might be mostly static, but I don't want to miss the Elusive Echo if I don't have to."

"Elusive Echo?" Ashe asks.

"It's a kind of radio game? They play a super ambiguous noise and then have people call in to guess what it is."

Ashe gives me an intrigued glance. "Have you ever guessed?"

I shake my head. "No, I usually listen on my way to work in the morning. It plays at noon on weekends though. But I've never had the courage to call. It's just fun to try to figure it out on my own sometimes."

Ashe shrugs. "Go for it," he says as he gestures to the radio.

I turn it on and twist the dial until I reach 94.1. There's a low hum before I hear a familiar voice.

". . . Elusive Echo . . . Sully . . . who is . . . caller?"

It's muffled, but the further we get down the road, the clearer it gets.

"Marth . . . happy to be . . . thank you."

"Are . . . ready?"

There's a loud thump and then a stretch of silence.

"You know what it is?" I ask Ashe.

"It sounds familiar," he says.

I laugh. "That's the point, I think. It could be a hundred different things. And you're always convinced you have the right answer. Then—"

The radio plays the classic four note pattern indicating the person guessed incorrectly.

"Better luck . . . time. Thanks for calling . . ."

I press the button to turn it off again. That's all I wanted to hear anyway.

"What do people get if they win?" Ashe asks.

"It depends," I say. "The longer it goes on, the bigger the prize pot. This one is just over two thousand dollars, I think? I can't remember. But it's been going for a long time."

"Two thousand," Ashe says under his breath. "For guessing a sound?"

I shrug. "Not the worst way to make a buck."

"Far from it," he agrees.

It's so easy with Ashe. It's like talking to a new old friend. And yet, it's so unfamiliar to me. The heat, the nerves, the heightened senses. If I didn't know any better, I would call it fear. But I do know better.

I look over to Ashe—clearly the cause of this swirl of emotions in my belly. The late autumn sun dances over his skin. His eyes are closed, and he's reclined back as if trying to absorb as much of it as he can. His arm is between us, relaxed against the upholstery. It's not quite an invitation, but it's not *not* an invitation either.

Slowly, I let my hand fall and reach over to his. Our fingertips kiss, and Ashe turns his head to look at me before finally wrapping my hand in his.

Our phones beep with messages as we come back into service.

"Care to check mine?" I ask.

Ashe puts his away before picking mine up. There's a long silence, as if he's trying to figure out how to work a touch screen for the first time.

"There's no passcode," I say. "You can just open it up. Actually, can you see if I have any messages from Mom? I should probably let her know about the cabin electricity as soon as I can so she can call someone."

Ashe is still quiet.

When I glance over, his jaw is clenched and he's looking at me with something I desperately don't want to see in his eyes.

"What?"

"L," he finally says, "I think you need to let me drive the rest of the way home."

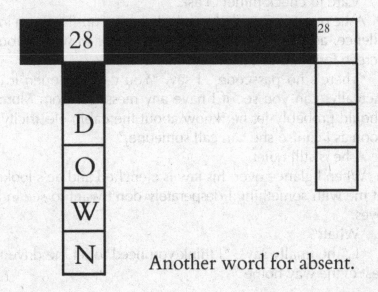

28

D
O
W
N

Another word for absent.

November . . .

"Breakfast is ready."
GONE.
DEAD.
Stale. Hot. Scratchy. Next step. Pain. Numb. Hollow. Music?
No. Silence. Sigh. Better. Peace.
GONE.
DEAD.
Alarm. Phone. Light. Ashe. Shame. Guilt. Down. Empty.
Dark.
Nyx. Nox. Purring. Rub.
Shuffle. Smile. Please. Thank you. Eat. Sick.
"This is the Elusive Echo."
Thump. Guess. Wrong. Sad. Next.
GONE.

E. A. M. Trofimenkoff

DEAD.
Shower?
No.
Brush teeth?
No.
Tired. Numb.
GONE.
DEAD.
Broken.
Meds.
Nyx. Nox. Cuddle.
Bed.

. . .

"Breakfast is ready."
Dry. Hard. Ouch. Stale. Late. Choke. Smile. Act.
"Just a bug."
"It will pass soon."
"So much to do."
GONE.
DEAD.
"I'll get out of your way."
Solitude.
Nyx. Nox. Pets. Purrs.
Alarm. Phone. Light. Ashe. Shame. Guilt. Down. Empty.
Dark.
Shuffle down the hall. Smile. Please and thank you. Eat. Sick.
"You have a visitor."
Mira. Jo. Vic.
Hugs.
"Yes, I'm doing well, thank you for coming!" Put today's
mask back in the emotional jar with the others.
Bed.

You and I Collide

"This is the Elusive Echo."
Thump. Guess. Wrong. Sad. Next.
GONE.
DEAD.
Shower?
No.
Brush teeth?
No.
Tired. Numb.
Broken.
Meds.
Nyx. Nox. Cuddle.
Bed.

. . .

"Breakfast is ready."
Chew. Swallow.
Buzzing.
GONE.
DEAD.
Dirt in my mouth. Smile politely. Excuse myself.
Shut the door. Breathe. Choke. I feel sick.
GONE.
DEAD.
Where is the sun?
My toes hurt.
Why are my eyes so dry?
Nox rubs up against my leg and meows at me.
Static.
Alarm. I pick up my phone. It's Ashe. Again.
Shame. Guilt. Empty. Dark.
I shuffle down the hall and put on a polite smile. I remember
to say please and thank you. I eat. It tastes like food.

"This is the Elusive Echo."
Thump. Guess. Wrong. Sad. Next.
Shower?
No.
Brush teeth?
. . . maybe . . .
Sigh.
Okay.
Tired.
Meds.
Nox nuzzles into my armpit. Nyx beside her. Their purrs fill
the silence. We cuddle.
Bed.

. . .

"Breakfast is ready."
It's sweet. Strawberries with cream. On light fluffy pancakes.
Warmth. The first real breath I have taken in days.
Gone.
Dead.
"It's nice to see some color in your cheeks."
"Life in your eyes."
I politely smile back.
"Thanks for breakfast, Mom."
Shower.
I missed the water.
I scrub and scrub and scrub until my skin is bright pink.
It feels good. I close my eyes and lean my head against the
cold tiles. Hot water down my back to wash away the pain.
The past.
I brush my teeth for the second day in a row.
Hair up or down? Probably down. I don't need a tension
headache on top of all this as well.

Deep breath.

"This is the Elusive Echo."

No one ever guesses correctly. Why do I even listen to this?

Introductions.

Thump.

Another wrong guess.

"We'll be back tomorrow!"

Mom's in the kitchen. It smells wonderful.

"Hashbrown casserole," she says. "Yes, again. I know it's a comfort food for you. And, well, we could all use some of that these days."

I give the twins their favorite treats. Nox leans against my leg, depositing a generous amount of hair in return.

What would I do without her?

Without them both?

"Thanks, Mom. I love you."

"I love you too."

. . .

My normal clothes feel weird over my skin. Like a hug from a familiar stranger. Has my body always looked like this?

I stare at myself in the mirror. The dark rings around my eyes are striking against my pale skin. For the first time in my life, I regret not being even minutely competent at using or applying makeup.

Zombie aesthetic it is.

gone.

dead.

"This is the Elusive Echo."

I sit down on my bed and turn the radio up as I put my socks on.

Static. Introductions. Ashe. Jokes.

Ashe . . .

Ashe?

Clarity.

It is Ashe.

Thump.

I lean in closer. What could his guess possibly be?

"You really made this one as general and as specific as possible, didn't you?" he teases.

I smile. It's real. It's genuine. The first in days.

"We do our best here on 94.1."

Ashe laughs.

That sound. It's like hearing my favorite song for the first time all over again.

"Could it be . . ."

What is it, Ashe? What do you think it is?

"This is going to sound absolutely fucking bonkers, but . . . is it . . . someone getting hit by a door?"

Silence.

What?

Sounds flow through the radio speaker like coins falling on tile.

"Congratulations! You've just won the prize fund! Now, I must ask you, what gave it away? Or was it just a lucky guess?"

Silence.

My chest throbs. My face is wet. Am I . . . crying?

"Let's just say I have some experience," Ashe says. "And yes, that does make me a lucky man, indeed."

I grab my phone from the side table. My heart pounds in my ears. The darkness is still there, but I can finally feel the sun on my skin again. The screen lights up, and although I can barely make out the letters on the keyboard, I finally respond to Ashe's messages.

"I'm the lucky one."

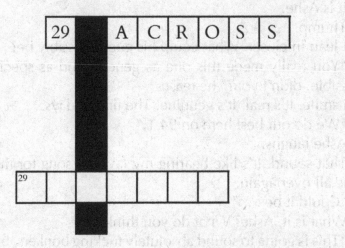

| 29 | ■ | A | C | R | O | S | S |

| 29 | | | | | | |

Tu me manques, you are
_ _ _ _ _ _ _ from me.

November 23, 2024

The woman's lips are far too red. She's trying to say some-thing, but I can't hear her over the distraction of the speck of lipstick that somehow found its way onto her front teeth. It doesn't matter what she says or how long she talks, the dots persist, almost taunting me.

"L?" my mom asks.

I shake my head. "What?"

"The lady would like to know if we have a flower prefer-ence."

"Oh."

I swallow and drop my gaze down to my hands that are folded in my lap. I anxiously tug at a hangnail, pulling it loose. A small dot of blood grows from the wound. The sharp pain grounds me. But I still don't have the heart to respond. This woman doesn't know me. She doesn't know us. She definitely didn't know him . . . my Pops. She doesn't deserve to know his favorite flower. None of them do. That was only for us.

Us.

Just me now . . .

Just me to remember how his face lit up every birthday when I brought him his simple, plain white carnation in a fishbowl. Just me to remember how he watered it every day and diligently attended to its plant food. Just me to remember that he kept it alive weeks past when it should have expired. He was tenacious.

But not tenacious enough.

"There was something he used to love, but I can't quite remember," my mom says, a hint of embarrassment in her voice.

My chest throbs.

It's so unfair.

All of it.

But he was her dad. And she's asking for my help.

"Carnations," I say under my breath.

"What was that?" mom asks.

"Carnations," I repeat. "White carnations. With baby's breath."

Mom lets out a sigh of relief, and I think the red-toothed woman asks something else, but I don't care. I'm all out of . . . well, everything. I'm just numb. Maybe it's better this way. You can't crash if you're not moving.

Mom signs a few papers, and I nod every once in a while, to make it seem like I'm paying attention and engaging, but I am really only brought back to my senses when we're back home and Mom hands me a small folded piece of paper.

"What's this?" I ask.

"We read the will earlier today. This was addressed specifically to you," mom replies.

She brushes a hair behind my ear and presses the letter into my hand. "You don't have to read it now if you don't want to, but I'm going to get out of the car, so if you want, you can have some time alone, okay?"

I nod, but don't take my eyes off the parchment. It's sealed with his classic full moon wax stamp. I run my fingers over the familiar bumps and grooves.

"Okay," I finally say.

"Take all the time you need."

Mom closes the driver's door and makes her way up to the house, leaving me alone with only my thoughts, and this one last piece of my Pops. A part of me never wants to open it. Maybe, if I leave it sealed, it will be as if none of this ever happened.

But would you rather live in a world of "what-ifs"?

I sigh, break the seal with my thumb, and try to ready myself for whatever words he might have for me.

My dearest L,

If you're reading this, then I have done what I never hoped to do . . . what I know will inevitably happen anyway. I don't know what finally got me, but I sure as hell hope it's a story worth telling. And if it's not, just do me a favor and make it one, will you? It'll be our little secret. Well, yours, I guess.

Point is, kid, I'm sorry. Knowing you, I'm sure you're beating yourself up over everything you said, and over everything you didn't. And since I know you so well, I know that anything I say here won't be able to convince you to stop it, so I won't try. Instead, I'll just say I forgive you. Not that there will be anything to forgive, I'm sure, but regardless, I think you'll need to hear it. If you can't forgive yourself, I'll do it for you.

Being your Pops has been, and I'm sure will continue to be, the greatest adventure of my life. There hasn't been one single moment where I have not been proud of you. I'm sorry I didn't tell you often enough. Hell, even if I told you every day, I still would have fallen short. Sometimes there just aren't enough words. Or perhaps the issue is that there are too many.

I know you'll want to find the bad guy in all of this, but promise me you won't make it yourself. Blame the universe, or entropy, or chaos, or something. You can't fight the natural order of the world, kid. And as it turns out, neither can I. It looks like neither of us was a match for time.

I learned this lesson far too late in life, but perhaps I can save you some time and grief in learning it on your own. The world isn't like those books you love. You don't need a villain in order to be the hero of your own story. You're enough. Just you. Just as you are.

I took the liberty of changing my will when you were just five years old. I don't know if you remember or not, but you told me that you were going to rule the world from the cabin's living room one day. And who am I to hold you back from that dream? It's all yours, kid. Give 'em hell. Show 'em the taillights.

One day, I know we'll find our way to each other again. Until then, you know where to find me. I'll see you on cloud nine.

Love always,
  Your Pops

My eyes fill with the tears I have refused to shed over the last few days. I hate crying, but maybe if it's just between Pops and me, it's okay. And I know it's not a super sad time. Pops lived a full life: over eighty-five years of highs, lows, laughs, and heartbreaks. Am I allowed to cry for someone whose life wasn't taken unexpectedly or before their time? Surely it must be more of a celebration to make it to his age, but then again, at the same time, he had so many more days to bond with us, to love us, to make his irreplaceable spot in our hearts. Would it have been easier to lose him years ago?

I dismiss the thought as quickly as it came. No. I wouldn't trade the years we had together for anything, not even for the cracks in my chest that must surely be threatening to split me in half. No. Not even for that. This feeling that seems to be bubbling in me like a volcano about to erupt is just the love that I can't pour into him anymore. At least, not in the same way. It has no physical place to go, and it feels wrong to just let it go and release it back into the universe. Just like . . . chaos.

I laugh. The sound comes up garbled and awkward, but the sobs soon turn to hysterical giggles and suddenly the tears that trickled down my cheeks turn into waterfalls. Can I not think about the science of things for just one fucking second? I know Pops would get a kick out of this, so I force myself to just accept the insanity of the moment and pretend as if he's here laughing beside me. In a way, it's like saying goodbye. One more laugh. One more good cry. One more moment.

And just as it always does, that moment ends as swiftly as it arose, leaving me once again feeling empty and spent. Tomorrow, we will have a moment again. Perhaps our final one, as we say goodbye one last time.

November 24, 2024

"As you probably know, my father wasn't a man of faith. He grew up in a Christian household, but he stepped away from the religion shortly after moving from home at the young age of nineteen. Just a few months later, he met the love of his life, Giselle, my mother. They shared over fifty years of love, which included eight houses, three kids, seven dogs, and one very special grandkid."

My heart pangs in my chest as if I had been punched. Mom's gaze meets mine over the eulogy paper she holds in her shaking hands. Her eyes glisten with unshed tears that threaten to spill down her face. I clench my hands into fists, feeling every indent of my nails into the tender flesh of my palms. I can't lose it here. Not now. Not surrounded by everyone. And not because of some fear of being perceived as weak. No, I abandoned that a long time ago. This comes from a much darker place. If I crack, even one more inch, everything will come crashing down, and I'm not sure I will be able to pick up the pieces after. At least, not with everyone else around.

"After Giselle passed away, Harry was lost. He described it as 'losing all of the stars in the sky within a single breath.' Day after day, my siblings and I were helpless. We watched him waste away in front of our very eyes for weeks. Until L came by and, like what often happens with them, said the right thing at the right time without even knowing it."

A sob catches in my throat and I press my fingers deeper into my palms, trying to distract myself.

Keep it together.

"Can I hold your hand?" Ashe asks.

I shake my head. Every inch of my skin feels as if it's being prodded at by a thousand tiny needles. I can't. I can't take any more.

"I'm sorry," I manage to choke out.

Ashe gives me a warm smile.

"It's okay," he whispers.

"L came home from University that weekend, excited about some kind of dynamic and couldn't wait to share it with us. I'll be honest . . . I didn't understand any of it. But they did. And it somehow breathed a new life into Harry. It was a magic that I never thought we would see in him again, and yet there it was."

Mom sniffles and wipes her nose with a tissue. A symphony of shuttered breaths and sobs echo through the small hall. Each sound is like a knife through my brain, telling me to just give up and let it go.

"As I was going through his things, I came across a leather journal that my father kept with him. I never saw him write in it, but I saw him read through its pages a few times. Whenever I asked him about it, he would just say, 'It's something that helps me get through my days, and especially my nights. One day, you might just need it as well.' And so I found myself on the floor of his room, blanket wrapped around myself as I read and read and read. But they weren't his words. They were L's. And since they were so powerful to our dearly loved Harry, I can safely imagine that he would wish them to be shared with you all today. Perhaps they will help get you through the night as well."

Mom reaches down and grabs the worn leather journal from below the podium. The soft *whoosh* of the pages as she flips through finally pushes the first tear from my eyes, unleashing the storm brewing behind them.

"Dear Harry," Mom starts, "it's Harry. Today I learned about the universe and its rules and laws. I learned about energy and waves and a great deal of many other things that I probably couldn't pronounce, let alone spell. It turns out that, yes, indeed, this old man can still grow and learn, and perhaps more importantly, live. L showed me a light in a darkness which I didn't know I was surrounded by. And what was that light? Entropy, as I believe they called it, the natural order of things: disorder. We are all small agents of chaos in our own ways—vessels of infinite possibilities and futures, capable of complex decision-making, and that in itself is a small miracle. But it struck me that even though life felt incomplete, it was, in a way, the most complete it had ever been, for in order to truly be complete, one must get to the end. That is the natural order of things. The cycle. It is as natural to end as it is to begin. And just as I marveled at the births of my children, and when I first held baby L in my

You and I Collide

arms, so too must I appreciate the beauty in such a fulfillment of the circle of life. So, Harry, if you feel as if you must believe in something to hold you through the darkness, to soothe you through the night, let it be this: the cycle continues, the wheel turns, the Earth spins, the grass grows and dies and grows again, and with every new generation comes change, and, most importantly, the endurance of hope. I do not know if one day I will see Giselle again, but I hope that whatever energy she has returned to the universe recognizes mine after I too transcend this mortal realm."

I don't know when, but at some point during Mom's reading of Pops' journal entry, I buried my face in my hands and began to weep. The tears bite at my eyes as I look up and meet Mom's gaze. She wipes her cheek with the back of her hand before addressing the crowd again.

"Thank you all for being here. You are welcome to join us for a brief lunch. And if any of you have any stories or memories you would like to share with the family, we have a few pens and a new leather journal for you to use near the front entrance. Take care, everyone."

What am I supposed to do now? My body won't listen to any of my commands I try to give it. It won't stand. It won't smile. It won't even squeeze my hands anymore. All I can do is breathe and try to ignore the pounding in my chest that is echoing through my ears. I'm vaguely aware of Ashe offering me his hand, looking down at me with red eyes and blotchy cheeks.

How did I get here? I'm in front of a table lined in black cloth filled with plates of pastries and open-face sandwiches. Pops would have hated that. He always despised open-face sandwiches. Especially the tuna salad sand—yup, there they are. Disgusting.

My legs carry me forward with the line. A few people tap me on the shoulder, and I fight not to wince from the contact. I know they mean well, but could they not just leave me the fuck alone? Plus, everyone, including myself, is a snotty mess right now. What a perfect storm for an evil virus to come and wipe every single one of us out. I make a mental note to wash my hands several times before consuming anything.

The food tastes like ash in my mouth.

Ashe.

Oh fuck, where's Ashe?

I whirl around in my chair and find him making his way back to our table.

"You OK?" he signs.

I swallow and nod, although I doubt it looks very convincing.

When Ashe finally takes his seat next to me again, he rests an arm on the back of my chair, but not close enough to touch me.

"I'm here," he says.

Somehow, I know that he doesn't mean he's here physically. He means that I'm not alone. And even though I find that impossible to believe, there's a small part of me that holds on to that fantasy for dear life.

"I'm glad you're here with me," I tell him. And I mean it with every fiber of my being.

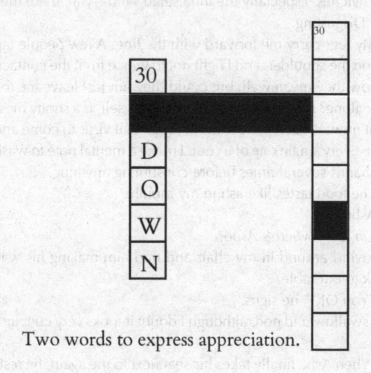

Two words to express appreciation.

November 25, 2024

The smell of freshly baked snickerdoodles floods my senses.

What a week . . . what a month . . . what a year.

Ashe hums to himself as he transfers the cookies onto the cooling tray. There are no words to describe how grateful I am to have him in my life. It was as if I was wearing mismatched socks my whole life, only to stumble and find that perfect fit. Life was fine before. It worked. But now everything feels as if it's finally fallen into place.

Except for the one missing piece that will forever be out of my grasp.

Mom said that Pops' heart condition had worsened and that the medications were starting to impact his kidney function. The day he collapsed, they were on the phone making sure that all of the paperwork was in place. That there wouldn't be anything to worry about, formally speaking, if something were to happen to him unexpectedly. He put Mom's name on his bank accounts and life insurance plan and who knows what else. That's what he was telling her that day. And they agreed to keep it between them. Pops wanted to live out the rest of his life knowing that people saw him for who he was, not a living dead man.

When Mom first told me, it felt as if I had been robbed. Maybe I could have said something more, given an extra hug, told an extra joke, anything . . . But then I realized that I would have seen him in the light that he had never wished to stand in. And so wishing that I had known and being angry for being kept in the dark wasn't fair, despite the fact that the anger was so much easier to hold on to than the grief. I had to let it go. I could feel guilty for leaving, for not being there and not being able to say goodbye. Or I could forgive myself, like he said, and find a new kind of peace in life.

"Snickerdoodle?" Ashe asks.

He holds out the pale cookie on a plate to me. There's still a hint of steam coming off of it.

"Careful," he says as I reach for it. "It's still hot."

I hold the cookie between my thumb and index finger and give it a gentle blow.

My eyes land on the crossed-out list on the fridge, the red ink absentmindedly scratched through the series of words that brought us together. "Who would have thought that a list like that would have brought us here," I say.

Ashe hums in agreement. "Well"—he leans against the counter as he takes a cookie for himself—"in the spirit of applying and completing the scientific method, what were the results? Did the experiment work?"

I let out a long breath and take a bite of my cookie, thinking as I chew. Images of laughter, whimsy, curiosity, and something else that makes my stomach feel warm from more than just the baked goodness flood through my mind.

"In the moment? Yes . . . But right now? I'm just tired," I admit. "It's hard to feel anything except the empty space in my heart where he used to be."

A new wave of guilt washes through me. Once again, Ashe is here, offering me support and compassion, and I'm just babbling on about how dark and desolate I feel. But . . . no, that's not quite the whole truth. There is something else, a slow and steady thrum of affection. And although it takes some focus to access it around my grief, it's still there. It's shrouded by a shadow for now, but it's like gazing up into an overcast sky: even if you can't see the sun, you still know it's there, waiting for the clouds to part so that you can bask in its brilliance once again.

"Are you sure this is okay?" I ask him.

He nods. "I want to be here, I promise."

I take a few more small bites, trying to coax my body into accepting his care and compassion.

"I'm sorry I never replied," I tell him. "I should have apologized soon—"

"You have nothing to apologize for, L," he interrupts.

I suck in a breath as he takes a step closer to me.

"Can I hold you?" he asks.

I swallow and give him a small nod.

Ashe's arms wrap around me in a now familiar embrace. He smells like cinnamon and sugar. I want to bury my head into his chest and never come back up again. If it were possible to physically live in someone's heart, I would choose his a thousand times over.

"My love is not fragile, L," he says into my hair.

Ashe's grip tightens around me and I sink into the embrace, letting his honey-sweet words melt around us. "It's not something I give lightly anymore. It's a choice I make every day because I want this. If the world was ending, where would you want to be? Because I'd want to be here. With you. Beside you. Wrapped in your arms as you tell me about some random space or science fact that might save us. I choose you, L. I want to spend every happy day laughing with you, and every sad day drying your tears. I want you to ignore my messages when you don't have the energy to reply. And I want you to trust me to love you through it anyway."

Tears fall hot from my eyes to my cheeks, making small wet patches on his black T-shirt.

"What can I say?" Ashe pulls back and grabs a tissue. He wipes away my tears from my wet cheeks and smiles down warmly at me. "Sometimes the universe speaks in riddles, and sometimes it hits you in the face."

The room is brighter than I remember it being before. Maybe it's just me. The colorful feelings tree reaches its branches out proudly from behind Iris like wings. It used to scare me before, but now it feels like an old friend reaching out a helping hand.

"Congratulations," Iris says as she stands from her chair and moves around her desk.

"For what?" I ask as I blow my nose for probably the thousandth time this session.

She hands me a new box.

"You survived the unsurvivable."

I look up at her with scratchy, swollen eyes. Her soft, familiar smile feels like I've been showered by the late spring sun. It fills me with a sense of hope—the promise of a new leaf, a new dawn, a new breath of fresh air.

"I shut down," I admit, embarrassed. I turn my gaze back to my tearstained hands.

"And yet you're here, L. That's no small victory. You don't give yourself enough credit."

Iris' words echo Pops' as they float through my mind. Maybe they're right. At any rate, what would be the harm in trying?

"Thank you," I choke out.

Iris takes a seat in her normal corner chair and crosses her legs. "You've lived your whole life waiting for the other shoe to drop."

I wince at her words. She's right.

"It's your brain trying to protect you, so please don't be upset with yourself. But here we are. The shoe is down. We're in the mud. But you're not alone."

I think of my friends who came to see me every day after Pops passed. Who I could barely manage to look at, let alone speak to. They didn't judge me for it. They just wrapped their arms around me, holding me, holding space for me, even though I didn't know how to ask for it.

I think of my parents, especially my mom, who no longer has hers. Who processes her emotions by cooking, cleaning and helping others.

I think of Ashe, who never once has given me a reason to doubt him. Who has trusted me with his past, his mistakes, his insecurities, and most importantly: his heart.

"No," I agree, feeling a sense of cold calmness settle under my skin. "I'm not."

Like snow from a fire.

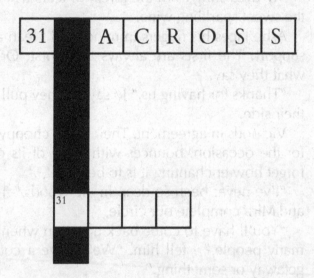

31 | A | C | R | O | S | S

31 | | |

December 24, 2024

The cabin feels empty this year, despite being physically packed full with my friends, my parents, my aunt and uncle, and, of course, Ashe. Yet, the Christmas tree doesn't quite sparkle the same way, and instead of its usual liveliness, the space feels like settled dust. It's almost as if it too has come to the end of a cycle, and is resting, planting seeds, and getting ready for a new spring.

"To Harry!" my uncle says as he raises his glass of wine to Pops' photo hanging over the mantel. Beside it is the crossword paper crane. I finally opened it up and completed it a few weeks after he passed. The last clue was "three words for my favorite grandkid." The answer of course: I LOVE YOU.

I think he knew, even then, that it might be his last puzzle.

"To Harry!" we all chant, holding our drinks high in salute to this man whose presence will forever be absent from here on forth.

My eyes sting from the threat of tears as I swallow down the sweet sparkling wine.

Ashe laces his fingers in mine, and I lean against him for support. The firsts are always the worst. Or at least that's what they say.

"Thanks for having us," Jo says as they pull Vic in close to their side.

Vic nods in agreement. Their short, choppy hair, dyed red for the occasion, bounces with a life of its own. "I always forget how enchanting it is to be here."

"I've never been so deep in the woods," Tony says as he and Mira complete our circle.

"You'll have to come back up again when there aren't as many people," I tell him. "We'll have a couples weekend getaway or something."

Tony's dark lips twitch to the side. "As long as it's not hide-and-seek in the forest, I'm okay."

Mira rolls her eyes. "You watch too many movies. The worst we'll do is tie you to a chair and force you to have a movie marathon with us."

Tony's eyes widen and we all laugh.

"Don't worry," I tell him, "we usually wait until the third or fourth visit before that ritual."

The look on the man's face is priceless.

Ashe's grip tightens and he turns me around to face him. "Mind if I steal L away for a minute?" he asks my friends.

After they all give their permission, Ashe leads me outside. It's a beautiful, clear night. The stars seem to blink at us against the velvet black sheet of the sky. I shiver from the cold, and Ashe wraps an arm around me.

"I needed some air," he admits.

I lean into him. "I don't mind."

A blissful and peaceful silence settles around us. The muffled voices from the people inside seem to fade away until there are only the two of us.

"I did it," Ashe says. "I texted Zander."

My chest fills with a now familiar warmth. "And?"

"He wants to meet for coffee in the new year." Ashe's words come out light, as if held on the wings of hope.

I lean further into him. "I'm so proud of you," I tell him. And I am. I truly am.

I reach into my coat pocket and find the folded paper that's been sitting there for the last week. I've been waiting for the right time to give it to him, but I've always found a reason to back out. Maybe now, here, where it's just the two of us in this place that holds so much love and memory . . . maybe here, we can make and share one more.

"I have something for you," I say, trying to muster up as much courage as I can.

I carefully bring out the paper and open my palm, extending the gift to him.

Ashe lets out a feathered breath. "Is that . . ."

"Open it and find out."

Gently, Ashe takes it from my hand and coaxes the corners of the paper outward, revealing the crossword puzzle.

"I know it's not much, but—"

Ashe's lips press against mine, hard and passionate. His arm wraps around my lower back to pull me closer to him. I bring my hands around his neck and lace my fingers in his hair, deepening our kiss. Seconds turn into minutes. Minutes turn into years. Time ceases to mean anything anymore. Right here, right now, nothing else exists. Only him. Only me. Only us.

When we finally pause to catch our breath, something catches my attention from the corner of my eye. Ashe must notice it too because his head turns at the same time. The night glows with the life of the northern lights dancing across the sky in brilliant shades of green.

"Beautiful," Ashe breathes.

He moves his hand around my waist and pulls me in. I rest my head on his shoulder as we watch the swirls of light swim through the night.

I'm not sure I'll ever be whole again. At least, not in the same way. A part of me will always be missing. But I've gained someone as well. And maybe that's what life is: the ebb and flow of love in all of its forms. A new cycle, ready to begin.

THE END

THE END

Thank you for reading *You and I Collide*. I hope that Ashe and L's story was just what you needed to believe in love and find joy in life again. Remember to take care of yourself, and know that you are always surrounded by love, even if it doesn't feel like it.

Zander's story is up next in this interconnected standalone series. If you would like to stay in the loop on other releases, please consider signing up to my newsletter (www.eamtro-fimenkoff.com). You will get first access to merch drops, reveals, giveaways, promotions, sales and more. Looking forward to having you!

AUTHOR'S NOTE

There were so many places in this book where I felt like I was the one being read and written, not the other way around. Writing is inherently a vulnerable practice, but this was on an entirely different level. In so many ways, this is a love letter to my fellow queer and neurodivergent siblings who are also working through their own brain blips and story arcs. We're all a work in progress. I think it's important to remember that doing your best looks different from day-to-day. Some days you can take on the world, learn a new language, and bake dozens of cookies, and on others, sometimes it's all you can do to get out of bed. If you need to hear it, I see you. I recognize you.

I hope L's story feels like a warm hug. I hope it makes you believe in yourself and the goodness in the world again. But most of all, I hope it allows you to love and appreciate yourself a little more.

In case you're wondering, yes, Claresholm is a real place. It's a small town in Southern Alberta. All of the places mentioned in the story are also real. There actually is a giant yellow airplane at the end of fourth street. If you're ever in the area asking for directions on the west side of town, there's a good chance people will use that as a landmark. Golana Books in this novel is inspired by two of my favorite bookstores: Analog Books in Lethbridge, Alberta, and

McNally Robinson in Saskatoon, Saskatchewan. Analog features an incredible intimate setting, complete with AMAZING staff and the cutest bookstore tabby cat, and McNally has this really cool giant tree with a spiral staircase going around the trunk that I just HAD to include.

Here are some of the other real and inspired places mentioned in *You and I Collide*:

The Hawk — inspired by The Owl in Lethbridge, Alberta

The Video Place — real, but sadly closed back in 2016

Flowers on Fifth — inspired by Flowers on 49th in Claresholm

Paul's Place — inspired by Roy's Place, and yes, they do actually have giant cinnamon buns

Centennial Park — real, but the waterfall feature is actually from my other favorite park in Lethbridge

The Fox Den — inspired by Old Fox, a restaurant that closed many years ago. There is a similar business in the Arena though!

The Lion's Park — remember the scene with L hanging upside down on the monkey bars? That scene takes place at the Lion's Park in Claresholm, and, yes, that exists too.

ACKNOWLEDGEMENTS

I think it goes without saying that this book wouldn't exist had I never met my lovely partner ten years ago. Ashe and L's meet cute was inspired by ours, but nothing can truly compare to the moment we first met. That magic is something that can't be replicated in words on a page.

I also wouldn't be here without the love and support of my friends and family. You know who you are. I love you all dearly and am so thankful to have you in my life. I specifically want to give a special shout-out to Harper-Hugo, Will, and Tamika. Y'all's friendship means the world to me, and please believe me when I say you make the world a brighter, better place.

It is no surprise that Pops is inspired by my real-life connection to my grandparents. I am so lucky to have known all of them, to love them, and to be loved by them in return. I wouldn't trade our memories together for anything. I am truly blessed to be your grandkid.

To my beta readers: Cathrine, Lauren, Rachel, and Randi, thank you so much for helping me make this story what it is! To my street team: Aidyn, Jaira, Kass, Kaylee, Megan, Molly, Sabrina, and Van, y'all are amazing. Thank you for being such a great group of people to work with. Thank you for the hype and excitement. But most of all, thank you for believing in me.

To my good friend and proofreader, Rebecca, thank you so much for being a literary wizard. I always learn so much from your edits and advice, and can't wait to work with you on future projects as well.

To my amazingly talented friend, colleague and interior formatter, Cathrine: I don't think I need to tell you how much I appreciate you since I do it every time we speak, so instead, let me tell you how cherished and loved you are for just being you. Thank you.

To my fur babies, thank you for interrupting me every single chance you could. This book wouldn't be the same without your insistent aaaaaaaaa edits from stepping on my keyboard. Thanks for keeping my word count up. All jokes aside, I love you guys. But do you really need to keep leaving fur deposits everywhere? You're never going to read this anyway. It's just a losing battle on all fronts.

Finally, I want to give my sincere appreciation to Analog Books for all of your support. Seeing my work on your shelves has been a dream come true, and I'm so grateful that y'all were willing to take a chance on me.

SNICKERDOODLE
RECIPE

1 cup of butter   (in a separate bowl)
1 1/2 cups of sugar   3 tbsp sugar
2 eggs   3 tsp cinnamon
2 3/4 cups of flour
2 tsp cream of tartar
1 tsp of baking soda
1/4 tsp of salt

- warm the oven to 350 degrees
- mix butter, sugar, eggs in a bowl
- combine flour, cream of tartar, baking soda, salt
- mix all together
- cool in fridge for 10-15 minutes

- using a medium scoop, roll dough in sugar and cinnamon mixture
- place on non-greased cookie sheet and bake for 10 min
- remove from pan right away and cool on racks

CROSSWORD
ANSWER KEY

1. MIND
2. DARK
3. COLLIDE
4. FRIENDS
5. MELANCHOLY
6. INTROSPECTION
7. CHEMISTRY
8. MYSELF
9. FAMILIAR
10. JOY
11. BUCKET LIST
12. CAT
13. NATURE
14. QUIP
15. LEARN
16. TRADE

17. DIFFERENT
18. EXPERIMENT
19. BOOK
20. FALL
21. MEET
22. PAINT
23. COURAGE
24. CETUS
25. ATTRACTION
26. INTIMATE
27. COFFEE
28. GONE
29. MISSING
30. THANK YOU
31. ASHE

ABOUT THE AUTHOR

E. A. M. Trofimenkoff (they/she) is a Lord of the Rings and cat enthusiast from Southern Alberta. When she's not doing research, writing papers, preparing presentations or teaching chemistry, you can find them writing fiction (obviously), binging TV shows with their partner, re-reading The Hunger Games for the 30+ time, or pestering one or more of their four cats. If it's not any of the above, she's probably sending memes. Good luck catching up on the days' worth of material she's sent you since you started reading this book.

Author photo is by Jordan Tate
(jordantatedesign.com, @t.a.t.e._ on instagram).